I0631224

Byron J. Rees

Trumpet-Calls

For the unsaved

Byron J. Rees

Trumpet-Calls
For the unsaved

ISBN/EAN: 9783337315481

Printed in Europe, USA, Canada, Australia, Japan

Cover: Foto ©Andreas Hilbeck / pixelio.de

More available books at **www.hansebooks.com**

TRUMPET-CALLS

(FOR THE UNSAVED.)

BY

BYRON J. REES,

Author of "The Heart-Cry of Jesus," "Christlikeness," "Hulda: The
Pentecostal Prophetess," "Hallelujahs from Portsmouth Nos.
2 and 3," and Review Editor of "The Revivalist."

Cry aloud, spare not, lift up thy voice *like a trumpet* and shew my people
their transgression, and the house of Jacob their sins.—ISAIAH LVIII: 1.

M. W. KNAPP,

Publisher of Pentecostal Literature, Office of The Revivalist, Pentecostal
Holiness Library, and Full Salvation Quarterly,

CINCINNATI, OHIO.

Copyright, 1899, by M. W. Knapp.

TABLE OF CONTENTS.

THE FOREWORD.

The author is becoming more and more impressed with the brevity of probation. The world may stand for a thou- The Passage of Time. sand years or for ten thousand— of that we know but little: *our* part in it, however, will soon be over, our destinies will soon be fixed; our opportunities forever gone. "We never look upon the same river," and our opportunities are floating past us never to return. What we do we must do quickly. God is striking the horologe of time; the shadow on the dial of life is ever shifting. Swifter than the Empire State Express, than the flight of a Mauser bullet, than thought itself is the passing of Opportunity. Our trains are all hurrying toward the one great terminus, Eternity, and it behoves us to take heed lest we be deposited upon the station-platform utterly unprepared to leave the cars.

But how much does that man owe his fellowman who has been awakened to the awfulness of sin and the bliss of heaven? Can the saved man do anything less than his very utmost to save men and yet keep his soul clear from the blood of damned souls? If those fortunate lepers who chanced to discover the Syrian spoils had neglected to spread the glad news in the starving city all history would have hissed and cursed them. The spirit of Christ's Gospel is altruistic. No sooner is a man truly saved himself than he springs to his feet on fire to help someone else.

Our Duty.

> "Bless me, Lord, and make me a blessing,
> I will gladly Thy message convey;
> Help me to help some poor needy soul,
> And make me a blessing to-day."

The Master said to His disciples, "Lift up your eyes and look on the fields, for they are white already to harvest." A "white harvest"! We have seen the restlessness of the Western farmer when his wheat was "dead ripe." We have heard him say that if his grain was not harvested

The White Harvest.

soon, the wheat would shatter out of the "heads" and go to waste. What anxiety must there be in the heart of Jesus, the great Husbandman, as He sees precious souls falling to the ground and the great waving field of standing grain yet untouched by the reapers.

Shall we not enter into fellowship with Jesus? Shall we not be in sympathetic touch with the lone Man who prayed until grey dawn on bleak moun- *The Lone Man.* tain peaks? We can do but little ourselves, but we can do our best, and at that Christ always smiles. Was there a richer reward ever bestowed than that which fell to the lot of Mary? "She hath done what she could."

We must not be discouraged by the greatness of the task. We must remember that having done all we can do, our *Unwavering Faith.* duty is to leave all else in the hands of God. A man can never be too eager for the triumph of right, but he may be too impatient. Let us have a strong, unwavering faith in Jesus, and with calm, rock-ribbed earnestness *"cry aloud and spare not and lift up the voice like a trumpet, showing the people their transgressions and the house of Jacob their sins.''*

The purpose of this book is to warn men against sin and its consequences, and lead them to Scriptural penitence and full salvation. The author enters upon the service of writing this message conscious of one thing—a burning desire to help save men from sin and hell and heartache and misery and wretchedness, and point them to a Christ who can and will bestow cheer and happiness and laughter and consolation.

A Burning Desire.

It is our prayer that these pages may be read thoughtfully and prayerfully. Do not read for entertainment. You will not find it. Read for benefit and blessing, and God will give them.

Benefit and Blessing.

Sinner, if you should find between the covers of this volume a coat which fits you, do not pass it on to another. For the sake of your own soul, for the sake of those about you, sturdily shove your shoulders into the garment made for you.

Your Own Coat.

It will protect you from the cold, deadly blasts of the winter of the Judgment.

Read this book to the glory of God. Satan, the aggressive, Argus-eyed enemy of your soul, would gladly persuade you *The Men of Berea.* to skim it lightly, laughing at its warnings and curling the lip at its earnest admonitions. Think seriously of your own spiritual welfare. Read, ponder, meditate, pray. Remember that the men of Berea "were more noble than those of Thessalonica in that they received the word with all readiness of mind and searched the Scriptures daily whether those things were so." If the slightest anxiety concerning your soul's safety arises in your mind cultivate it, encourage it, stimulate it, cherish it. It is a floating bough, such as Columbus found, pointing to a new world. It is a testimony that you have not committed the unpardonable sin and are not yet across "the dead-line."

O, brother! I cry to you out of my heart: *Make your peace with God. You* *The Steel Grip of Sin.* *have already waited too long. You* *have insulted God with your negligence and become the laughing-stock of devils, who plot your ruin. Flee to Jesus. Hide under the covert of His blood! Espouse Him as your Savior that you may shake off the steel grip of sin and shun the lurid path to the impenitent's hell!*

May the tender, loving Christ stretch His fair hands in blessing over us as we write and as we read. Amen! BYRON J. REES.

WESTPORT, MASS., 1899.

CHAPTER I.

FATAL INDIFFERENCE.

Never was the human mind so broad in its interests nor so wide-awake in its attitude as in this, the last decade of the century. There seems to be no limit to the catalogue of subjects to the study of which it stands read: to devote both time and energy in abundance. Whole departments of scientific studies are being opened up almost daily. New literary fields are being worked with enthusiasm. Invention goes forward with startling pace, and all the world gapes and wonders.

Modern Energy.

The mammoth printing presses of the modern publishing house make the wide diffusion of knowledge practicable and easy. The mill-operative is in a position to be a better read man than was the king in purple of a century ago. The high-school graduate of 1899 has studied more books and gained more information than the Harvard

Diffusion of Knowledge.

or Yale alumnus of the latter part of the eighteenth century.

Our interests are world-wide. Formerly only a very few took any interest in events *War and Invention.* outside of their immediate neighborhoods. Now all this is changed. The road-menders, eating their lunches in the shade, talk about Dewey and Manila and the Philippines and the happenings on the other side of the world. Nansen goes on a search for the Pole, and the eyes and interest of two hemispheres follow him. Hobson sinks the *Merrimac*, and "click, click," sounds the telegraph instrument and the news soon belts the globe and thousands of hands clap and millions of voices cry "'Rah for Hobson!" Edison toils and studies alone in his laboratory, but all the world is there with him, invisible, profoundly interested.

The multiplication of books, the growth of the newspaper, the increased facilities for *A Full Life.* transportation,—all these things help to fill the modern man's life to overflowing. Our forefathers had abundance of time on their hands. Sundays were always free for meditation and rest, while the evenings were generally spent quietly at home. This state of things was not without a moral effect.

When a man is alone, God talks to him. When he is out by himself with no business to pound on the panels of atten- God's Voice. tion, no magazines to make time pass swiftly, no book to bring him into touch with another's mind, then God sends His voice quivering down the air toward the unawakened soul. The first step toward a knowledge of God is separation from the whirr and roar of activity. If a man will but give God a chance, He will call to him.

Modern life crowds God out. Between the affairs of nations and the works of art, the adventures of explorers and Christ the pleasures of society, Christ is Crowded Out. crowded to the wall, and matters of eternal weight and moment are ignored. The "new books of the month," the drawings by Gibson, the latest novel by Kipling, "the Eastern Question"—all these have place in the heart and attention, but death and judgment and heaven and hell receive scarcely a thought.

The well-nigh universal unconcern in regard to matters so momentous as death and salvation argues the existence of a devil. Death is everywhere, and yet wise, careful, systematic preparation for it is rare. The great mass of people behave themselves as if life was eternal and the grave a mere myth, a mirage, a fancy, a figment of the brain.

Death.

According to social rules it is "not good form to discuss religious matters during a meal." Modern society is wearing blinders and goggles; not only that, but she regards with suspicion and enmity the man who would remove them. Religion and the ministers of Christ are held at arm's length. Even at death, when the kingdom of doom and despair is about to seize upon the impenitent soul, the anxious clergyman is told by the mother in the hall, "Miss Gladys is too sick to see you, sir. The doctor says we must not tell her or even hint to her that she is going to die." And

"The Poor Soul."

so, for fear of a momentary excitement, the poor soul slips off into torture and anguish.

Satan's plot can be descried in this systematic attempt to elbow God out of the life and heart. Hating the fair son of God with a sullen, persistent hatred   Razor-like Talons. he is determined to give Him all the heart-pain possible by damning all the souls on which he can get his razor-like talons.

It does not matter much to the Adversary with what he fills the life, if only he can exclude God and salvation. In some cases a demi-john and a tumbler are   Satan's Baits. enough, in others he must furnish a span of prancing horses, a black shiny coach and a cottage at the seaside. "If one bait will not tempt, possibly another will." This is his motto, and his whole course of procedure is in accordance with it. Some men can be damned with a pack of cards, but others go down more difficultly. In some cases, all Europe must be ransacked for rare pictures by the Masters and all the world searched for fine scenery, lest the soul be surfeited and turn to God.

A certain German Professor could be caught with no less bait than an exhaustive study of the Dative Case. Esau sold his birthright for a mess of pottage. Poor Poe wrecked his soul for the pleasures of dissipation. Solomon grieved the Spirit and poisoned the kingdom with polygamy. Some split on the rock of ambition, others on the reef of the appetites, while still others are sucked downward in the black, noiseless whirlpool of worldly culture and refinement. A painting from Italy or a fine face, a name for learning or a position on a foot-ball team, the praise of acquaintances or the fear of scorn—it matters not with what the soul is hindered, if only Christ and the blood are debarred, Satan is satisfied.

"But I do not believe there is a devil!" Who, then, does the devil's work? Who is it that plants the goat-signed saloon on the corner, the harlotry in the alley? Who is it that turns sober men into raving maniacs, innocent boys into hardened criminals? Who is it that grinds

Rocks and Reefs.

The Work of Satan.

the face of the poor and breaks the hearts of wives and mothers? Who is it reddens the plains and harbors with blood and fills the earth with the sound of blows? Every black deed of ghastliness and crime, every dying sinner crying, like Goethe, "More light! More light!" every betrayed girl, with her face buried in her hands; every neglected orphan crying in the cold, every bastard cursing his despised parent, every sigh, every groan, every tear, every wail, every sin, argues the existence of a devil.

Supposing you do not believe in the existence of a devil, does your unbelief do away with him? Skepticism destroys nothing except faith and "The Federal Express." your own hope of salvation. You may doubt that strychnine is deadly in its effects, but if you take it it will kill you. The other night our train was plunging across New Jersey, through a dense fog, at fifty miles an hour, when suddenly the brakes were applied and the train came to a full stop. The brakemen seized their lanterns, ran back on the track a short distance and picked up the mangled body of a man. The unfortunate fellow did not *believe*, doubtless, that walking the track was so dangerous, but in an instant the iron thunderbolt struck him and his blood spattered the wheels of the locomotive.

After all, it is probably not a matter of much concern to Satan as to whether or no **"A Myth!".** we believe in his existence; all he wants is to get us. It would seem on the whole that he is glad for us to deny his existence. How grimly must he smile to look over the shoulder of one of his disciples and slaves and find him hard at work on a magazine article entitled, "The Devil: A Study of the Development of a Myth!"

There is no appeal from "Thus saith the Lord" for honest men. The Bible invari- **Eternal Facts.** ably takes for granted the existence of the devil, and what God takes for granted in talking to man, man is a fool to doubt. It were not more foolish to butt our brains out on stone walls than to dash our souls into shreds on the rock bulwarks of eternal facts.

Satan is the Arch-Deceiver. He is compared to a serpent, a nocturnal sower of tares, a wolf. With sly cunning *The Devil's Chain-Gang.* and secret attempt he is hoodwinking and blinding myriads of souls all over the turning world. The heathen worship him as a god; civilized nations deny his existence, yet bow down to him in the form of selfishness, greed, and mere intellectualism. Tireless and ubiquitous he is shackling and manacling millions of wrists and ankles, handcuffing and fettering untold hosts of souls, driving them in his chain-gang down the smoke-grimed crater into hell.

CHAPTER II.

THE CONSCIOUSNESS OF GUILT AND SPIRITUAL POVERTY.

Why should a man think least about that which concerns him most? Because his *A Bound Mind.* mind is bound by the Prince of darkness. Yet so many things *ought* to make the indifferent sinner halt in his tracks, aghast and thunderstruck at the horror of his condition!

The *consciousness of guilt* is universal, and ought to make a man reflect, consider his *The Voice in the Soul.* ways, and alter his course. When a man puts himself to the point of query, and asks himself, "Do I ever feel guilty?" he is compelled to answer in the affirmative. There may be whole days when the sense of condemnation is not experienced, but suddenly a voice sounds in the soul, "Thou art condemned and deservest punishment." No sinner can say truthfully, "I do the best I can." The *least* that can be

20

expected of him is that he give his heart to God and cease his sinful course. God has put in the soul a gun which can not be spiked. It is *Consciousness*. From its red-hot grape and canister there is no permanent relief except in Jesus. "I feel guilty" is the sentiment of all impenitents, whether they express it or conceal it.

No amount of argument and theory can silence the cry of consciousness in the heart. Supposing some smooth-talking preacher *does* say, "There is no Hell; that word ought to be relegated to the speeches of gibberish old women and tales of the nursery;" supposing a backslidden church *should* decide that the New Testament representation of eternal punishment is only a liberal use of mere figures, a horrid dream, a phantasy, a nothing, *nothing would be altered in the matter of consciousness.* Though infidelity and apostasy should clasp hands, swing hats, and shout, "No Hell! No Hell!" something within the breast would say, "If there is no Hell, there ought to be one, for I have sinned and deserve righteous penalty."

There Ought to be a Hell.

If there is no Hell, where will God put the hopelessly impenitent? If a man shuts his
The Gaol of the Universe. eyes to light and grinds his teeth in hatred of God and righteousness up to the very last, can there be a Heaven for him? God never forces the will, never compels men to be good; such "goodness" would not be goodness; it would have no moral quality. Hell is the gaol of the Universe and into it are turned the "wicked and all they that forget God."

A man can not get away from himself. Guilt dogs his steps; unrest palsies his facul-
Macbeth. ties until his best works are only shadows of what he might do were there no disturbing cry in the heart. Guilt sees retribution in everything. Even God becomes an Avenger to the eye of the condemned soul. "Macbeth sees Him with forked lightnings without and volcanic fires within," because blood is on his hands and conscience.

A man is built for nobler things than this world can furnish. There is a hunger in the heart that nothing material can satisfy. The first-cabin passengers who leave the *Majestic* at the pier after their Summer in Europe have that same un- Nobler Things. satisfied look in their faces which they had when they left America in the Spring. It is not with travel, nor books, nor scenery, nor money, nor learning, nor friendship, that the immortal spirit can be fully satiated. As St. Augustine says so beautifully in one of his prayers: "O Lord, our souls were made for Thee, and they are restless till they rest in Thee."

Would God build a temple for Himself and then refuse to live in it? Would He erect an edifice with halls and chambers A Deserted House. fit only for the divine Shekinah and yet not fill the emptiness of the house?

There is nothing sadder than a deserted house. The writer when in school frequently passed one the rich owner of which had left closed and uncared for Loneliness. while he traveled in the Orient. The arched gateway covered with untended ivy, the grass-filled walks, the closed shutters, the smoke-less chimneys, the air of loneliness and desertion which filled the place, all told the passer-by that the house had lost its tenant.

Supposing that the house is human and sentient; supposing that when the owner

*An Argu-
ment.*

and lord is absent it pines and sickens; supposing that its lord is the Lord of Heaven, would He leave it to the mercies of time and age and light and darkness and heat and cold and rain and ice? No; the fact that there is an indescribable yearning in the soul for God is an argument that God will dwell in the soul if it will permit Him.

God knows that nothing less than His presence can ever make us permanently

*A Yawning
Chasm.*

happy. Look at that great yawning chasm in the heart! Will you fill it? Then hurl in the Pyramids of Egypt! Is it full? No. Tumble in a row of tenements, a business block, a name for wisdom and culture, an unexcelled popularity. Now is it filled? No! No! These things fall so far in the gaping crevice that we do not hear them strike! Empty in the Alps and the Rockies and the Himalayas and the Con-

tinents and all the world! But the void is
not filled! What *can* fill it? GOD only.
When He enters in, the aching emptiness is
gone and the soul becomes "complete in
Him."

CHAPTER III.

THE STARVING HEART.

The heart is greater than the brain. Erasmus was a thinker, but Luther was a lover of

Erasmus and Luther. men's souls. One was clear and cold as ice; the other flamed and burned with a passionate affection for the salvation of his fellow-beings. One quickened the intellectual life of Europe, but the other was the Father of the Reformation.

When a man espouses Christ, he lets his heart have liberty. The sinner locks his heart

An Imprisoned Bird. in an iron cage against the bars of which, like an imprisoned bird, it beats with bloody wing.

Not infrequently a man has become so devoted to literature and learning that his

"If I Had Known." heart has starved to death. Carlyle buried his heart under piles of MSS. and lecture notes; harshness crept into his manner and raspiness into the tones of his

voice until finally he broke the heart of the fair, trustful girl whom he had promised to love and cherish.   Friends used to find him at her grave murmuring, "If I had only known; if I had only known."

The people who have blessed us and thrown light into our lives have been "people of heart."   Brilliant **Unselfish Devotion.** men are admired and talked about, but to them we do not turn in hours of grief and loneliness.   Goethe was more of a scholar than Schiller, but the latter is beloved by a nation while the former is studied chiefly by literateurs. Very rarely do men really love the scholar who gratifies his thirst for knowledge by hiding in the cloisters of some gray old university, but nations sing the praises of Florence Night- ingale and Jenny Lind and Clara Barton be- cause they had sympathetic hearts and placed their talents at the service of the people.

"Give thy heart a chance, O man!" cries Wisdom.   Let the gentle songster **The Gentle Songster.** go free.   It longs to leave the cruel cage, pierce the blue sky and dart back and forth in the free, open air of heaven. If you keep it encaged, all your hopes for this world and the next are destined to die.

A pastor in Wilkes Barre, Pa., told me of an accident which occurred near that city.

A Mining Accident. One afternoon there was a bad "cave" of slate and coal, and six men were imprisoned by the fall of hundreds of tons of the black rock. Attempts were made at once to rescue them, although it was the opinion of the oldest and most experienced miners that the men were already crushed to death.

Day after day the work of excavation went on. Meanwhile, the six men, shut off from **Starving in the Dark.** all means of escape and forced to consider the thought of an awful death, faced the danger as bravely as they could. One of their number was chosen leader. He divided the oil and food, using the greatest care to make fair apportionments. One lamp was kept burning a few hours each day; the remainder of the time was spent in utter darkness. Food was soon exhausted, and one of the mine-mules, which was on the point of starvation, was killed and eaten. One day they heard the faint sound of distant blows. Hope sprang up in their hearts and the sounds of the rescuing party came nearer every hour. At one time, as the workmen outside rested for a moment, they heard almost inaudible sounds from below; they were the signals made by the prisoners. They were starving in the dark, with little hope, and no power to help themselves; but they were signaling for help.

It is thus with a man's better nature. It is imprisoned by landslides of sin and gigantic "cave-ins" of iniquity. It is *Audience and Succor.* starving, crying in the dark. It makes pitiable, inarticulate signals of distress praying for audience and succor.

O man! man! give your heart a chance! Do not deny it longer. You have choked it, strangled it, throttled it for *The Crushed Heart.* years. Let the Savior head a rescuing party for its release and liberation that, like the rescued miners, it may breathe the open air.

CHAPTER IV.

THE SHORTNESS OF LIFE.

Another cause for immediate reflection and thoughtfulness is the shortness of life. The *Life's Brevity.* average length of the human life is so strikingly short! There are comparatively few old men. Look at the throngs who jostle and hurry on the street, study the faces of the traveling men in the hotel, search hard to find aged men who are teachers or writers; one can not but see that the great mass of men die and are buried before they reach middle-life. Disease in some one of its million forms, or war, famine, over-work, worry, grief, heart-ache, cyclones, tornadoes, epidemics, sewer-gas, wrecks, disasters, all these carry men off with celerity. A cold, a rusty nail, La Grippe, a hearty meal, a fractured rail, a broken stirrup, a misstep, and in a trice the name is taken off the door-plate and placed on a grave-stone.

30

Where is the man so idiotic as to say, "I am planning to die impenitent!" You can not find him. Ransack the Big **Repentance Put Off.** Cypress Swamp and hunt out the old hermit living on roots and ask him if he intends to go to death without repenting and he opens his eyes wide and stutters, "No; I believe in a Superior Being and mean to make my peace with Him." Accost a blue-coated policeman and question him about his chances when he himself is brought into Court before the Judge of all the earth and he will say, "O, I mean to die a Christian." They all *mean* to die Christians, but only a few do.

"I will lead a better life sometime," said a dissolute fellow to an evangelist, but the days glided by like skaters on the **"Sometime."** ice and in a sudden hour the miserable man was hurried up to the docket of omnipotence and omniscience to meet life-accounts kept by a celestial book-keeper.

Youth is the period of Spring, of hope, and of courage. The young man looks forward to years of vigorous life and green laurels of

success. He does not give possible accident,
or disease, or death a moment's

Fell Dead.

thought. Time slips by like mercury fleeing from grasping thumb and finger. Grey hairs whiten the temples of the busy God-forgetter, wrinkles furrow his brow, care makes haggard his eye and cheek; he is forty, then forty-two, then forty-five; he is thinking of having his life insured. One day the ambulance halts in front of his door, and four men carry a still form up the steps. "Fell dead in the office" explains the driver to the maid who opens the door. The unapparelled soul of a negligent sinner has gone to meet the God he slighted and forgot.

Life is so mercilessly short. The thought falls back upon us again and again, like pebbles thrown upward against the

A Procrastinator.

face of a precipice. We were holding meetings in a city in Pennsylvania. There was a man in the audience one day who was the subject of much solicitude and prayer, but he seemed hard and callous. As he left the church, the pastor, a very godly man, felt profoundly impressed, as he watched his retreating form pass down the aisle and out the door, that the man would be dead before night. He could not rid himself of the impression. He even mentioned it at the dinner table an hour afterwards. At two o'clock, word came to the church, "Geo. Pierce fell dead a few minutes ago!" He had resisted God for the last time. He had counted on a length of life and a multiplicity of opportunities that were denied him.

It is strange we do not reason about death as about everything else. That we are all compelled to die some time no one will deny. After the famous Sheer Insanity. doctor has done his best there will come an hour at last when things will grow dark and unconsciousness will creep over us like fog over a landscape. What folly, then, to dismiss the thought of death from the mind! What sheer insanity to refuse to consider the problems of the grave and another world!

We remember the King who presented his court fool with a staff, saying: "When thou

findest a greater fool than thyself give him
the staff." The King fell sick.
The medical men looked grave
and said: "He can not live!" The fool
stood by the bed of the dying ruler.

"Fool, I am going on a long journey!"

"Art thou, my master? Of course thou
hast engaged rooms at the hostelries?"

A moment's silence.

"No, Fool, I have not."

"Then thou must needs take much gold
with thee to pay thy way."

"I have none that they will accept in that
distant country."

"How large a retinue will accompany the
King?"

"I am going alone."

"Will the King's friends in that strange
land receive him with kindness and love?"

"I have no friends there! They are all
my enemies!"

"What preparations *hast* thou made then,
O King?"

"None whatever! I intended to, but put

it off until it is too late. The journey now can not be delayed. I am forced to go !'

"How strange! Ha! Ha! Here, Sir King, take the staff! It is thine! Thou art greater fool than I, though I wear cap and bells!"

What greater folly is there than for one to neglect preparations for death until it is too late!

Walk down the street. Yonder is a flag of black crape dangling at a door-knob. Some day that dark emblem will hang at your door and mine. Look at that hearse, with its ghastly urns and sable, shining wood-work. A hearse will one day carry you and me to our last resting-place.

Crape.

O careless, flippant, jesting man, there will come a time when you will not jest. There will be a morning when you will not rise and go about your habitual work. Towards noon, perhaps, the doctor will drop in. A few days more and telegrams will summon relatives. A day more, and rallying from stupor, you will see that the room is filled with people, perceived but dimly, with handkerchiefs to their faces.

The Coming of Death.

The doctor will hold your wrist in one hand, his watch in the other. The room will darken; a face grinning like a skull and a form indescribable will appear before you. O, that shadowy form; and it will beckon you, and in spite of the skill of physicians, the care of nurses, and the tears and sobs of loved ones, you will follow into the rayless, pitch-black Eternity of Torment!

Death is coming; shall we not prepare for it? Every man has his choice between two kinds of deaths. He can die the death of the wicked or the death of the righteous.

Two Kinds.

A few of us stood about the bed of a dying saint in central Indiana. The day was drawing to a close, and the shadows were darkening in the corners of the room. It seemed to us that a light fell about the head of the bed. What triumph and victory filled the countenance! There was no fear, no struggle, no twitching of the face. A child dropping to sleep could be no calmer. The placid, beautiful soul slipped out and away to the Garden of God.

A Saint's Translation.

CHAPTER V.

THE JUSTICE OF GOD.

There is yet another reason why the impenitent man should arouse himself from his lethargy, rub the sleep out of his eyes, and take action at once. *God is just*, and this fact ought to make every sinner shiver and fear.

An Awful Fact.

We sometimes hear it said by shallow, unthinking persons, "Oh, well, God is a just God, and will give us no more punishment than we deserve."

"Than We Deserve."

"Than we deserve!" Ah, right here is the difficulty. What we "deserve" is precisely what we ought to fear. Have we not broken the righteous law of a holy God? Have we not neglected, spurned, scoffed at the Savior of the world? Have we not despised His ministers and neglected His Word? Have we not sinned in secret and in public? What we "de-

The Only Course Open.

serve " is ceaseless torment in the Peniten-
tiary of the Universe, and that is the penalty
which a *just and holy God must* impose upon
the finally impenitent.   There is no other
course open to Him.   His nature is such
that He must act along the lines of exact
equity and rectitude.   Men who have spurned
the blood of Christ and deafened their ears
against His voice, must go into "outer darkness where there is weeping and wailing and
gnashing of teeth."

Let us be assured of this: God will mete
out to us the exact and particular penalty
The Celestial   which belongs to our lives.   Our
Surveyor.   lives with their hills, valleys,
milestones, stiles, prairies, and plateaus will
all be measured and surveyed by the Celestial Surveyor, whose clear and accurate mind
will ferret out all the hidden things and
make the little sins of the yesterdays appear
as they are, blacker than a cloudy midnight.

Aye, aye, sir, God is just.   Do not fear
that He is not; tremble rather because He is.

Drowning men rescued at the last moment
frequently behold the ghastly array of the

sins which they have committed drawn up before them. Every volition is recorded somewhere, and it lies The Tribunal of Heaven. in the power of illuminated memory to bring us face to face with every deed of our lives. When we step up to the tribunal of heaven, if we can not plead the blood of Jesus, there will arise before us, like the apparitions of armed heads and bloody children and marching kings before Macbeth, all our jealousies and envies and lusts and uncleanlinesses and filthinesses, a sad army forcing from us the piteous cry, "Undone! Undone!"

Ought we not give these things some thought? Do they not concern us more than the latest novels, the fashion plates, Worthy of Thought. a fine horse, an armor-piercing projectile, the cathode rays, a rare book, an European composer, a brawl with Spain? Is not the soul and its salvation of more importance to us than anything else in the world?

CHAPTER VI.

THE WILL OF GOD REVEALED.

God has revealed to us His attitude toward sin. There can be no doubt as to how God regards sin, for He has taken the one satisfactory way of enlightening our minds about it. He has made a *revelation*.

A Revelation.

Without a direct revelation, man is always a poor, groping, struggling, blinded creature, with no knowledge, and no prospect of any except by divine intervention. God gave Greece and Rome excellent chances to work out a natural religion. What was the result? What were the "high religious conceptions" evolved from the national consciousness? Jove was a tricky old profligate, the gods made a harlotry out of the human race, and the whole religious system reeked with filth.

Greece and Rome.

In philosophy, no definite concrete re sults

were obtained. " Plato alone, of all the Greeks, reached *the vestibule* of truth and stood upon its *threshold*." Philosophy. No one found out the way of salvation. The great mass plunged onward, laughing at the thoughtful, and even *they* fought vainly with their doubts.

Without a direct revelation, we are undone, and undone forever. A religion which spurns divine revelation breeds Offal and selfishness, pruriency, and moral Refuse. leprosy. Take the God part out of a sermon, out of a book, out of a prayer, out of a world, and the rest is offal and refuse, fit only for burning.

And yet we are forever emphasizing what man does. We laud *man's* colleges, *man's* culture, *man's* science, *man's* art, and speak of God only when neces- Conceit. sary. It is natural for us to love to talk about ourselves. We are never quite in our element until we are telling some one about what *we* can do and what *we* know. This is because we are self-centered and conceited— the theological word is "depraved."

With all our self-laudation, we are a poor, miserable, hell-approaching race, and ought

Charcoal and Lightning. to always paint our future in charcoal and lightning if we desire a truthful picture. High and low, opulent and poverty-stricken, Webster-brained and base-browed, we are all on the same road toward the same destiny, except as we hide under the covert of Christ's blood.

God made direct revelations to the saints of the Old Dispensation. Enoch and Abram

The Chief Revelator. and Moses and David and Isaiah and Daniel, these men talked and walked with God. To them, with many others, God showed Himself and His plans. Then Christ came, God's great and chief Revelator, and men saw more clearly than ever before the heart of God. Gradually the fund of God's imparted truth accumulated, and the result is—the Bible.

"But I do not believe the Bible," says some small person. Indeed! Then Satan is

Eternal Instinct. wiser than you, for he "believes and trembles." You *should* say that the statements made by the Bible are *unwelcome*, and that you *hope* they are not true. For, after all, there are few who do not believe the Word of God. Theoretically, many are infidels, or atheists, or Deists, or what not; but, when put to the test of storm or death-bed, eternal instinct rises up in panoply and acts on the orthodox basis of faith in the divine government and the revelation of God as seen in the Bible.

Head infidelity is usually heart iniquity. The saloon-keeper professes to disbelieve the Bible, because if he admitted that he believed it true, he would Professed Doubt. be compelled, if consistent, to knock the bungs out of his beer-barrels, wash the gutters with "rock and rye," and invite Salvation lassies into the bar-room to hold a prayer-meeting.

Would you find the chief cause of doubt? Probe in the heart. The physicians probed the body of Garfield in search of The Cause. the bullet, but they failed; but no sooner does the keen instrument of careful observation touch the heart than, lo, the cause of unbelief is discovered.

The explanation of the modern wave of Old and New Testament criticism is to be found in the spiritual lapse of the church. When a man's heart loses God out of it, he begins to be "filled with his own ways," his own theories, his own prejudices. The modern higher critic comes to the Bible professing to revere "the scientific method," shaming the more conservative into silence or consent by his trumpeted frankness in searching for "facts." But, as a matter of observation, the critic is committed to a theory before he opens his *Biblia Hebraica*. His decision is a foregone conclusion.

Higher Criticism.

The latter-day critic has frequently won himself an audience more respectable than that of his brother, the blatant infidel, by hanging out a sign, "In the Name of Science," and yet nothing is more unscientific than the methods of study pursued by these glib dealers in "Elohistic and Jehovistic documents." As has been pointed out "science consists in the exact observation of certain facts according to the

The Name of Science.

following accepted principles: (1) Facts observed, not assumed; (2) facts as observed, without prejudgment; (3) consideration of all relevant facts; (4) no forcing of facts, whether by rejection or insertion; (5) logical inductions from the whole body of facts, unhampered by theories, unconfuted by grave exceptions; (6) substantial agreement on the inductions; (7) conclusions that exclude conflicting explanations."

The higher critics violate every one of these principles. Wellhausen and Kuenen entered upon their study of the Old Testament Scriptures with a

Kuenen.

fixed "determination not to accept the supernatural." They are therefore incompetent judges of such a library of books as the Old Testament. Kuenen says: "So long as we allow the supernatural to intervene in even a single instance, so long our view of the whole continues to be incorrect."

The result of all this unscientific twaddle and soft-speeched infidelity is a

Mr. Andrew Lang.

Polychrome pertinently: "The method [of the Bible! Mr. Andrew Lang says higher critic] is simple and Teutonic. You have a theory, you accept the evidence of the sacred writers as far as it suits your theory, and when it does not suit, you say that the inconvenient passage is an interpolation. It must be, for if not, what becomes of your theory? So you print the inconvenient passage in green, I suppose, or what not, and then the people know all about it."

So far as we have observed, the theories and methods of the critics pretty much agree. Driver and Cheyne, and Harper and Smith are all of the same sceptical stripe, and are all embarked in the same boat; although, of course, not all do the same work. Some steer, others pull the oars and watch their more favored brethren who steer. They humbly hope they too may sometime "take a turn at the wheel."

Critics.

So long as the mind, the thinking nature, is not kept in abeyance to a spiritual and devout heart, so long there will be wild, foolish theories and "isms." Until we really want "to do justly

Insane Doubts.

and to love mercy, and to walk humbly with God," we will be the butt of the ridicule of demons because of our insane "doubts."

And so let us remember that the mistakes of Moses are not half so much in our way as our own sins. Men of clean *Joseph Cook, Etc.* heart and strong, vigorous brain believe the Bible. Joseph Cook, William Ewart Gladstone, Jonathan Edwards, Abraham Lincoln, George Washington, Daniel Webster, Louis Agassiz; these are the kind of men who pin their faith to the Word of God and risk their souls on the veracity of the Book of Books.

God's Word is true. It has stood the blasts and billows of centuries, and like a strongly-built sea-wall, it still *The Bible Remains.* breasts the giant seas unmoved, immovable. The Voltaires, the Thomas Paines, the Rousseaus, the Madame de Staels, the sceptics and doubters and jeerers and scoffers have gone, or are swiftly going beyond this life, but the Bible lives and grows in influence every day.

Some one has compared the Bible to a

marble cube. Some self-blown infidel tries

A Marble Cube. to "upset the Bible." Long years he strives. But sooner or later, whatever his name, Strauss, Renan, or anything else, Death lifts up a bony hand, and pulls him underground, and the cubic Bible, four-square and eternally complete, is as symmetrical, solid and safe on one side as another.

And there is something in the soul which corroborates the Bible's claim to being the

Blasphemer's Conscience. expressed will of God. After the most wordy mouther of scurrilous blasphemies has left the lecture platform and gone to his room at the hotel, there is something within the mind which says, with a leer, "Now, look here, that is all right for making money, but, ha! ha! ha! *you* and *I* know better. It is all very well to make those thick-skulls cackle and laugh, and feel safe from Death and Hell and Judgment for a minute, while the hand-clapping goes round the room, but, pshaw! you simply *know* there is a God and a Hell, and you are on the way to a place of misery this very night." And the man turns on his pillow and tries to sleep, but he knows the voice is right. Thank God for these voices which invite and warn and expostulate and entreat, making it possible for a man to seek and find the Savior.

CHAPTER VII.

GOD AGAINST SIN.

However difficult it may be for us to understand some parts of the Bible, one
<small>Both Balm and Vitriol.</small> thing is sure—it is a book which forbids and denounces sin. From first to last, it is one emphatic protest against evil. It takes up all kinds, shades and degrees of iniquity and pronounces God's sentence upon them. While it is balm to the wounded spirit, it is vitriol and bottled lightning to the man who loves sin and is determined to retain it in his heart and life.

Christ is God's great Revelator. He is God projected into the world, making plain
<small>Magna Charta.</small> the will of the Father concerning our thoughts and actions, choices and lives. Take, for instance, the Sermon on the Mount, which is the Constitution of the New Testament Church. Notice how Christ attacks sin in this magnificent message.

One of the first sins which Christ singles out for condemnation is the sin of anger (Matt. v. 22). Of course His audi- **Anger— Murder.** tors knew that a man must be punished for manslaughter; but this fearless preacher astonished them by the startling declaration *that anger was equivalent to murder!* Ah, here is a teacher who goes deep into the heart, fearing no one and courting no one's favor. Anger is murder! "Then most of the murderers go unpunished." Exactly. Have we been angry with an unrighteous anger? If so, then we are red-handed murderers in the sight of God, and in constant danger, unless the blood of Jesus covers us.

Cast your eye over your shoulder and look at the years of the past. How frequently you have sinned this sin! You have **The Record-** doubtless been able to restrain **ing Angel.** your passion, influenced perhaps by the fear of consequences and the disgrace of exposure, but murder was in your heart, and the Recording Angel saw it and took note.

Another common sin which goes unrebuked in many parts of the country is that

Adultery. of adultery. Society abominates
adultery and seduction, and frequently manifests its abhorrence of these
crimes by violent measures. It is not uncom-
mon to find communities where public sentiment holds that three feet of rope or a heavy
charge of buck-shot are fit reward for the
scoundrel who violates the honor of womanhood. But this indignation manifests itself
only against overt acts, while Jesus Christ
astounds mankind by the assertion that to
look upon a woman with impure desire is
adultery. Not only is the act of adultery
damnable, but unchaste desires and unholy
feelings are equally devilish and will meet
the same punishment.

The most discouraging fact concerning society is that, while it condemns sin by word

Hypocrisy. and profession, it commits it in
secret. The very people who would
be deeply mortified by a public cognizance of
their immorality are frequently low in their
conversation, vile in their thoughts and bestial
in their unseen lives. The woman who jerks

her skirts aside lest they come in contact with those of the street-girl, is frequently no better, morally, than her poorer sister whom she despises. To God they are all the same, and His justice respects no one's person.

In the 28th verse of the fifth chapter of Matthew, Jesus puts Himself on record as against all impurity. My dear reader, have you sin upon you? **The Curse of God.** Are you guilty of impurity of which you have never repented? Are there things covered which some day must be revealed to your infinite dismay and everlasting shame? Remember that all licentiousness, all lechery, all lewdness of thought or word or deed, call for the blighting, blackening, withering curse of Almighty God.

Profanity is a grave and common evil. "Thou shalt not take the name of the Lord thy God in vain;" said Jehovah, **Profanity.** and he who uses the name of Deity flippantly or as a byword is but whetting a knife for his own throat and sharpening a stiletto for his own breast. The disrespectful use of sacred words, the playful use of

holy exclamations, are all on the same plane
of guilt.   The sinner who cries out "Halle-
jah!" or "Bless the Lord!" in mimicry of the
voice of a child of God is simply inviting the
thunderbolts of God's wrath.

During a summer tempest there is a flash
of blinding light, and then a deafening crash,
Struck by Lightning.   and some one says, "The lightning
struck near here."   A traveler is
found beneath the shattered tree, his body
swollen and scorched, his hair singed, and
his eyes wide open and staring.   But his
death was due to a mere electrical discharge—
a plaything, a toy compared to the curse of
God on sin.

In the day of retribution, that awful day
when all but the blood-covered will weep and
The End of the Blasphemer.   wail, men will be struck by the
blinding, dizzying shocks of the
sky artillery.   Bloated with blasphemies,
with the oath hot upon their lips, they will
go down into eternal despair.   Unwelcome
though this saying may be, it is God's un-
changing truth.

One of the Ten Commandments reads like

this: "Thou shalt not bear false witness against thy neighbor." How frequently is this commandment **Lying.** broken! How easy it is for us to tell that about others which is not true. A few ladies meet for an afternoon tea, and before goodbyes are said a number of lies have been told and reputations permanently injured. Dr. Andrews defines a lie as a "willful intent to deceive." Many times there is a half-finished sentence, a sly smile, a laugh and a wink, and, lo, a false impression is made, a good name is injured, and a black lie is entered on the celestial books against the guilty person.

Gossip usually gets its spice and interest from falsehood. No wonder the Bible condemns tattlers and busybodies so **Idle Words.** severely. The Master said that we must give account *for every idle word.* One reason why the "church social" and the "church party" are such scourges to the work of God is because scandal and small talk and backbiting and falsification run rife on these occasions.

If you are not glad to see a person, for the sake of your own salvation, at least, do not

Be Frank. lie and say that you are. Do not ask people to " call again " if you do not wish them to; for in so doing, you are only practising deception and shadowing your own soul.

CHAPTER VIII

GOD AGAINST SIN—CONTINUED.

One of the greatest curses to America is the use of alcoholic liquors as a beverage. God's Word declares that no drunkard shall inherit the kingdom of God. **Liquor Drinking.** The man who is drunk all the time, and the "moderate drinker" who weakens his mind and fires his passions by his secret tippling, and all grades between these two men, are committing black crimes against God and their posterity and manliness and decency and all things noble.

Alcohol is the father of crime in thousands and thousands of instances. Children are born cursed from their father's **Cursed From Birth.** loins with a thirst for liquor, because their selfish parents drank "a little now and then." Look at liquor's harvests: Imbeciles, Convicts, Thieves, Blacklegs, Dwarfs, Scrofulous Systems, etc., etc. And who is

57

to be held accountable for this? He who breaks God's law and sins against his own body and offspring by the use of alcohol.

What havoc drink has wrought! It has made respectable men fit to consort with the The Havoc of dregs of society. It has changed Drink. well-intentioned husbands into brutes devilish in their unfeeling cruelty. It has made men beat the wives they professed to love. It has weakened the will and fired the brute in a man until manhood is dead and buried and only the wreck is left. Is there freedom from the power of habit and appetite? Yes, thank God! Lay yourself at Jesus' feet in utter submission and complete confidence in His power and willingness to save and deliver, and in the twinkling of an eye His voice will speak you free. Praise the Lord!

There is another crime of which many are guilty who do not know the taste of liquor. The Sin at the Indeed, many of our "best peoPolls. ple" are not free from the foul contagion. The hands of many of our preachers are red with this bloody sin. It is a sin

committed at the polls. The saloon-keeper
says, "May I sell liquor?" and the so-called
Christian bows his head, drops his vote, and
says, "Yes!" Are you a professed disciple
of Jesus Christ, and yet say "Amen" to the
liquor traffic? Shame upon you!

"Ah," you say, "but I must be true to my
party!" Indeed! "No man can serve
two masters," and if you are to
serve King Jesus He must have
precedence over your corrupt political party.

Party.

"Yes," says another self-excuser, "but
the issue is bi-metallism, and I must help
settle this." This is a mistake.
Satan is blinding the church's
eyes to the true issue. If she were to rise
up in strength, she could crush this accursed
traffic from the Isle of Shoals to the Golden
Gate, and do it at once, but she is hoodwinked
by political shysters, she is duped by keen
place-hunters, she is won by the siren voice
of "sound money," and the widows continue
to weep, and the daughters' hearts still ache,
and the children cry for bread, and the
prisons keep on filling, and the alms-houses

The Church's
Power.

increase in the land, all because the Church of Jesus Christ, bought by "the gold of His blood and the silver of His tears," casts a ballot for rum, ruin and damnation, and says to the saloon-keeper of foreign birth, "Go to, now, sell liquors and sink our sons in drunkards' graves and our daughters into dens of infamy; only see to it you give us license-money for the privilege we give you!"

"But I do n't want to throw away my vote." Look back at old Daniel. He

A Thrown-Away Vote.

seemed to throw his vote to the lions, but, lo, a little later, and he comes out to take a place beside the king and help run the kingdom. Jesus Christ seemed to throw away His vote, but He conquered sin and death and hell, and millions rise up and call Him "Redeemer." Better that we throw away our votes and keep clean than that we help swell the gangrenescent liquor count and pollute our souls with the slime of Hell.

Covetousness is a common and pernicious evil. It is variously regarded, but by most of people it is considered well nigh a virtue.

However men may look it, God forbids it and hates it.

To be wishing for some one else's money, to desire another's good fortune, to wish you owned the fine horses of your neighbor, or the commodious resi- **Worthy of Death.** dence of the man across the street, all this is damning sin, and worthy only of death.

Covetousness always causes discontent-ment. To be satisfied with what we have is truest wisdom, and always char- **Discontent.** acteristic of the fully saved heart. Remember that those whose fortune you covet are just as discontented as yourself.

Envy is a common and little grieved-over sin. Children are taught to envy those above them in wealth or social position. **Envy.** In order that the boy may save his pennies he is told that if he is saving, some time he can be a banker or a broker, and have plenty of money, and have other men work for him; and straightway the child is filled with envy of rich men.

God and man are ever labelling the same things differently. Frequently that which man considers desirable and estimable,

A Decayed Man. God condemns and abhors. Man makes envy half a virtue; God calls it "a rottenness of the bones." Imagine a man whose bones are decayed. The framework of all his system is rotten. Some day the whole physical house collapses and the putrid carcass drops into the grave.

Envy grows on one like leprosy. We begin by wishing for this and wishing for

A Growing Disease. that—cultivating a spirit of discontent. Gradually we get into the habit of scheming how to possess ourselves of another's good fortune, and slowly the envy-eaten man topples over and is gone.

It is wonderful how insidious envy is. Ministers envy their brethren their reputa-

Hellish Yeast. tion; church members envy some saint his name for goodness; a stammering man envies a fluent speaker his ready tongue, and thus the hellish yeast works and ferments and brings about damnation.

Cheating will bring to many a man Judgment-day pain and remorse. The really honest men are rare specimens, though there are plenty who plume themselves on being "fair and square," professing all things and possessing nothing.

How easily a man may glide into the habit of making money at the unfair expense of his fellow-man. Coal merchants who sell "short tons" for two thousand pounds, dry goods men who have dishonest measures, business men who pay their debts at forty cents on the dollar, and then live comfortably, will all have to meet the stern brow of inexorable Justice one of these days.

It matters not how we cheat, in what manner the unfairness is practiced, the guilt is the same. The man who rides on a single-trip ticket the second time through the oversight of a conductor is guilty together with the stable-scented jockey who swindles in a horse deal.

Equal Guilt.

The man who sells his time to his employer and then idles it away or spends it in looking out for his own interests, is a thief. He is supposed to be doing all possible in the interest of the man who pays

The Employee.

him, and he robs whenever he neglects his duty in any way.

The fact that a man is not paid as much as he thinks he ought to have, does not palliate "Common Thieves." his offense in case he steals from his employer. The conductor who "turns in" only a part of his fares, the errand boy who lounges along the street, the slippery bank defaulter and Ananias and Sapphiras, all belong to the same company, and when met by the face of Truth are branded by her white-hot iron: "Common Thieves."

CHAPTER IX.

GOD AGAINST SIN—CONCLUDED.

The employer who pays less wages than he can really afford to pay, is as much a robber as the red-handed bandits who in- **The Employer.** fest the caves between Jerusalem and Jericho. The principle upon which the world does business is, "Get all you can for as little money as you can," and that is a devilish, inhuman principle. If a man can not be a business man and be honest as heaven and clear as a sunbeam, he had better quit business. "But I'll starve!" Well, starve, then, if need be, but die an honest man.

But it is nonsense to suppose that business is necessarily dishonest. Thousands of Christian merchants and business **Christian Business.** men in the land rise up and tes- tify that dishonesty and trickery do not pay in business, and that Christian principles are the only principles upon which a solid business can be constructed. If the so-called Christian men on whose shoulders rest business responsibilities would conscientiously follow out the principles of the kingdom of heaven, in ten years all respectable and legitimate kinds of business would be in their hands.

The century which is just closing, however, has not been free from the gravest

Oppressors of the Poor. injustice and the most impudent arrogance on the part of capitalists. There are those who sit in cushioned pews, and give large sums for "beneficence," who grind the faces of the poor, murder fathers and husbands in poorly-ventilated shops, and stifle the babe and its mother in pest-house tenements. Students of sociology and slum-workers unite in saying that the condition of operatives is, in many manufacturing cities, simply disgraceful. You need not go far to find samples of the effect of greed for gold.

Visit the sweat-shops of lower New York with a policeman, and see for yourself. Look at the pale-faced mother making

aprons, stitching her very life into the garment with every turn of the needle.   "Annual
For whom is she working? A big   Apron Sale."
department store up town pays her a few
cents a dozen for making the aprons.   In a
few weeks there will be an "Annual Apron
Sale," when the shoppers of the city will
be "invited to look at some wonderful bargains."   And women with plenty of means,
but who are close and mean, and hard-eyed
and "shrewd," will buy aprons once wet
with the brine of a widow's tears, bedewed
with the salt tears of a woman as good as
they, or better, but one to whom the world
has shown a sour and bitter face.   But the
shoppers buy the aprons, and brag to their
friends about their "cheap" purchases.

"Cheap! Indeed, *are* they cheap?" says
Mr. T. M. Bateman, speaking of the cruelty
of cheapness. "They who feel a   Mr. T. M.
pleasure in purchasing articles for   Bateman.
less than the actual cost of production have
not the feelings of true, generous people, or
they would look at the other side of their
bargains, and they would think why they

were so cheap, and would remember that it
was the cheapness of death to some poor mor-
tal—death to her wages, to her happiness, to
her womanhood, to her health, to her hope,
to her body, to her soul!

"I brand this word 'cheap' as a lie, for
the article marked cheap will cost more
Starvation than the money paid for it. It
Wages. costs aching heads, burning eyes,
crooked fingers, tired limbs, breaking hearts,
many sighs and rivers of tears. The low
prices paid to sewing girls and factory hands
are fearful. A few pennies' pay for making a
pair of trousers, a waistcoat or a jacket! No
wonder that many, shrinking from bitter
poverty, barter away their virtue and take to
a life of shame."

God forbid that any of us should discover
when too late that our selfishness and pride
Our have wrecked some young life or
Selfishness. drowned some youthful battler in
the seething seas of sin and wretchedness.

Let us remember that sin is sin, and can
not remain covered. It will out at last to our
infinite dismay. God beholds sin, and no

thought, or desire, or feeling is hid from Him. The sin which no one knows but God and the sinner who sins will be dealt with as severely as the sin in a public square.

Sin is Sin.

Oh, the rottenness and putrefaction that fester underneath the feverish scab of appearances! There are men all around us fair in appearance, devilish at heart. They gain access into Christian homes, they move in "good society," yet their minds are putrid and vile. Slime and poison fill their minds, and their imaginings are soaked in lust. They are smooth men, these well-dressed Mephistoes, these unhorned and unhoofed devils; yet God's eyes pierce their mask, and their lechery and leprosy are as plain to Him as the type of this book. One may escape the hand of human courts, but the fingers of divine justice are like clamps of steel.

Slime and Poison.

Hypocrisy is the meanest sin that affronts God and mocks the pure heavens. It creeps upon society stealthily, like a crouching tigress. It is leprosy care-

A Crouching Tigress.

fully concealed by plasters and paint; it is small-pox rouged and hidden; it is Hell let loose in the night, and fevers spreading in the mists that lie on the face of the Swamp of the World's Evil.

One of the sins which hypocrites especially espouse is dancing. Have you not heard people say, "I see no harm in dancing"? THEY LIED WHEN THEY SAID IT. Any one who knows anything at all about dancing knows that it breeds lust, and awakens passions that make them of kin with the brute. Dancers know this. Only people foul at heart and gangrenescent in their secret life say, "I dance, and don't think it wrong." The woman who dances simply advertises her own pollution. Ten to one the wife who frequents the ball-room is faithless in heart to her husband and damns her own children before they are born.

Lustful Dancers.

Public sentiment is at last awakening on this subject, and even people who are not Christians are seeing the evil this filthy pleasure works.

Public Sentiment.

Is there a thing more inconsistent than to

see a grey-haired mother, a member of a church, defending dancing? She is simply saying to Impurity, **Impurity's Prize.** "Creep into the heart of my daughters, and turn their innocence into vinegar and fire. Capture the bodies of my sons, and drag them away to 'the house of the strange woman.'"

Chiefs of Police say that dancing fills the houses of ill-fame; slum workers tell the same sad story of dance-hall and lost virtue; sociologists who study **Lust's Furnaces.** crime report the same finding, and thus we are left without excuse. The indiscriminate familiarity of the dance can not but smirch the marble whiteness of the heart, and they who emerge from the sooty chimneys of lust's furnaces may imagine they are clean, but all the world knows their shame.

Objections of much the same nature debar the decent man or woman from the theatre. There may have been a time when the stage was a legitimate educa- **The Stage.** tional factor—certain good men claim this— but that day is past, and the average play of the present is such that no pure woman can look upon it without crimsoning.

It is the play filled with lewdness that makes "a good house." The faces of those

Irving's Practice.

who emerge from the theatre doors are the faces of people upon whom unbridled passion is doing its worst. Irving, the celebrated playwright, knew enough about the effects of theatre-going to forbid his daughters' attendance even at his own performances. But the sons and daughters of *church members* are allowed to attend these unclean exhibits unrestrained and unrebuked. Is it not true that "the children of this world are wiser in their generation" than the professed followers of the pure Christ?

Another sin which will not fail to damn men in the great Pay-Day is that of vulgar

Vulgarity.

conversation. It would be surprising were it known how many are guilty of this sin. The guilty ones would represent all classes, from the smutty punster who pollutes the society of the club hearth to the female gossip who sits at the tea table and discusses sacred subjects in an indelicate way. This blight of foul talk and loose conversation never fails to take all the fineness and delicacy from the soul. It corrupts and destroys all the taste for pure beauty and unsullied nobleness. Better that one make one's dinners from the garbage of the street than that one listen to the coarse tattle of low souls.

One cause for shunning "evil communications" is to be found in its effect not only upon ourselves, but upon others. The mother who says a word lacking in purity and elevation of moral tone before her child need not be surprised if she see her offspring become a prey to the most depraved and soul-destroying passions. The man who swears before his child lacks in both taste and sense. If he had better taste he would loathe swill; if he had more sense he would not pour vitriol into the soul of the child to scald the heart of its parent in later life. The truthful Christ, who can not lie, has said that we must "give account for every idle word." What did we say yesterday? How are we conducting the conversa tion of to-day ? It behoves us that we speak our words with care, lest out of our own mouths we should be condemned.

All sin is going to meet with justice at the hand of the Judge of all the earth. At the Day of Judgment, all the unrecog- nized criminals will be made mani- fest. All who have sinned in the dark and said "Amen" in the daylight, all who have professed one thing and lived another, all who have made official positions instru- ments of selfish gain, all who have incensed God with lies and falsifications, all who have made vows and have not paid them, all these God will judge in righteousness before the astounded universe.

Justice.

Let us not forget that GOD HATES SIN, and all the world is going to SEE ultimately that He hates it. We may not be convinced now. At present, the wicked, God-hating man may seem to thrive and flourish. *Apparently*, God favors the shyster as much as the honest man. Indeed, it sometimes seems as if integrity was re- warded by calamity. But these are only *ap-*

Unbiased Equity.

pearances. God is on the side of righteousness and will vindicate it at the last. God hates sin with an imperishable hatred, and there is no excuse that will shield the impenitent from the fury of His anger. The day will come when the immeasurable throng that shall stand before God's marble throne, convinced of His justice and unbiased equity, will cry out with those of Carmel, "The Lord, He is the God! The Lord, He is the God!"

CHAPTER X.

THE JUDGMENT.

It is very evident that there is a need of a general Judgment Day, a time of moral reckoning and divine penology. In the first place, the very complexity of human affairs demands a day when things shall be untangled. Our relationships are so numerous, so diverse and so complicated that only a divine and omniscient eye can see things as they are, and only divine wisdom can mete out rewards and punishments.

Complex Relationships.

A man's influence in the world does not end when they put his body in the cemetery. He has influenced every soul with whom he ever came in contact, and all the actions of his life have been a series of pent-up forces, whose power is boundless, immeasurable.

Pent-up Forces.

Voltaire is living to-day in his influences.

Look at the demonized face of the poor French infidel. His soul is get- Paul and Voltaire. ting redder every day with the crimson tide of lost souls. St. Paul is still blessing the world. The company of white spirits, who owe inspiration and help to him, is on the increase. A soul flashes into the world like a spark, burns awhile, dims, and disappears; but the light started by the moment's burning goes out across the silences of the Universe, and extends to the utmost boundaries of God's creation.

If a star was to go out to-day it might be years, yea, centuries, before the astronomers at the Lick Observatory would Drawing or Driving. notice any change. The light set flashing down toward earth ages ago is only just now reaching us. Though a man die to-day, his influence goes on until the Judgment, either drawing toward or driving from the Cross of Christ.

The effect of a life is incommensurable. You have a servant in your house. A Lost Opportunity. She performs her service, but you never speak to her about her soul's sal-

vation. She wishes you would, but your opportunity goes by and is lost forever. She
comes to have no respect for a religion which
is as selfish as yours seems to be. She has a
little son at home. She brings him up without prayer, without God. He becomes a
man, vile, blasphemous, filthy, drunken. In
a row in a Bowery saloon his throat is cut
from ear to ear. Who did the deed? The
man with the razor helped. Who helped
him? The prayerless mother. Who helped
her? You, *a professed follower of the Son
of God.*

Life is a tangled net. "No man liveth to
himself, and no man dieth to himself." All
the deeds of life are interwoven
and intimately connected. Many
a man owes his salvation to the prayers of
an obscure saint, who lived, fasted and
prayed two hundred years ago; and many a
poor fellow puts the pistol to his temple and
spatters his brains against the wall, who
was helped to the deed by a giggling, sim-
pering, unholy church member.

Goodness and badness spread infinitely.

A Tangled
Net.

A good deed will never die. The woman who anointed the feet of Jesus is to-day in the Paradise of God, **Ointment.** but the "odour" of her kind act "fills" not only "the house," but the Christian world.

"How far that little candle throws its beams !
So shines a good deed in a naughty world."

The life of Catherine Booth was filled with beautiful deeds. "When she lay in her coffin in Congress Hall," says **Catherine Booth.** Mrs. Morrow, "ministers, Members of Parliament and half-starved children of the slums were alike eager for a last look upon the face they loved. Roughs passed her weeping. Lost girls turned from her side and begged to be taken where they could begin to lead a new life. 'That woman lived for me,' a poor drunkard cried in anguish. They drew him aside, and on his knees he accepted pardon and promised that her God should be his.

"Three men knelt together at the head of her coffin one night and poured **"My Boys !"** out their penitence to God and went out of the hall saved. A tottering old woman stood so long looking down on the still, white face, that an officer gently asked her to move on. 'No, no,' she said, 'let others move on. I've a right to stop. I've come sixty miles to see her again. She saved my boys.' "

Such a life as Mrs. Booth's will never die. As the years lengthen into centuries, should our Lord delay His coming thus long, her life will only be accruing new rewards and more benedictions. Who can compute the good her life will do? God only, and at the Judgment she will receive a "just recompence of reward."

A Just Reward.

It is equally true that a bad life goes on rolling up a mountain of guilt and damnation fearful in height and weight. Yonder is a long sad line of dark faces and forms. They are in the gall of bitterness, in the bondage of death and despair. They have rejected God and hissed the name of Jesus in derision; but now, filled with foreboding and fear, they are called upon to meet the God of Judgment. And who is the man who heads the company and

Thomas Paine.

seems to have had influence over them? That is the author of "The Age of Reason." You remember that he himself, when dying, sought to have the book destroyed, but his infidel friends disregarded his last request. Behold the fruit of his life in these damned souls!

Who will be our Judge on that day? None other than Jesus Christ. The Christ whom sinners have rejected, the Lamb whose wounds reddened the earth at Calvary, the Savior and Redeemer of the world, will appear in a new office and perform a work vastly different from any He has undertaken previous to that time.

Jesus as Judge.

Oh, sinner, tremble! The meek and lowly Jesus, who stood so long at the door of thy heart knocking for admittance, is no longer calling thee to repentance. The day of repentance is past, and only remorse is thy heritage. Remember the occasions when, under the earnest preaching of God's Word, thy heart was touched. Those were thy opportunities; but Christ was put off with the words, "Not to-night."

Sinner, Tremble!

Recall the voice of the Spirit that fell so often upon thy ear and was unheeded. All that is past, and Christ is Judge.

Look at the Judge! He is no longer the scourged and tortured victim of Jewish hate **No Longer** and Roman brutality. He is not **Mocked.** now standing with bowed head before hard-faced Pilate. His face is neither pale with a death-like whiteness nor streaked with dried blood and spittle. His regal form is not mocked by the irony of borrowed purple. Nay, nay, not thus is He to be seen, but with eye of fire and form of God He rivets the gaze of all eyes and compels the reverence of all hearts.

To-day Christ is slighted and maltreated. Men do unto Him as they please. He is **The Slighted** ruled out of society and expelled **Christ.** from the boards of trade and ejected from the stylish churches ; but all this will be very different ere long. "Calm, level-headed business men" will writhe and welter under the iron feet of righteous retribution ; ladies of society, who pride themselves on their calm and undisturbed behavior, will in that day of fury scream like Bedlam and Pandemonium, while black-robed prelates and unfaithful preachers will long for death, and will not find it.

CHAPTER XI.

It is, of course, impossible for us to imagine the fearful character of the Day of
Judgment Terror. Judgment. After we have collected all the information concerning it which Scripture gives us; after we have taken into account the horrific nature of awakened memory; after we have reflected on the shaming effect of the revelation of all secret things, there remains to the Judgment a mysterious, nightmare-like terror that no mind can at present conceive.

It will be an awful day—a day of blackness and thick clouds; a day of anger and divine
An Awful Day. wrath; a day of final decision of destiny and the end of all probation; the focal point of all past days.

The end of earthly institutions will be seen when the throne of God is set; monarchies will crumble, and totter, and go

84

down in the mortar-dust of their own *debris;* democracies and great and grand governments will shatter like fine-blown glass, and the hearts of all men will tremble like leaves in the wind.

Like Leaves.

Oh, the disclosures of that day! Secret things will be revealed, unseen things will come to light. Reader, are you willing to have the secret work of your imagination emblazoned upon the blackboard of the Universe like stars on the flag of the Republic? Young man, do you relish the thought of your pure mother knowing the vileness of your desires? Oh, sad, sad hour for all who live double lives; for husbands who break the vows of matrimony and crawl into the sewers of filth; for wives for whom chastity and honor have no attraction; for deceivers and moral sleight-of-hand performers who bless with their lip and countenances, but slay and kill on the sly.

A Sad Hour.

Take, for purpose of illustration, the following incident, a single example of thousands like it: A gentleman on K—— Street,

in an Eastern city, a member of a large
A Popular "Christian." and fashionable church, has "an enviable reputation " for morality
and beneficence. His acquaintances and
neighbors respect and honor him. The
preacher, bland and suave, makes frequent,
prayerless calls upon his popular and influen-
tial parishioner, and, whether coming or
going, always smiles. He informs this important member of his congregation that he
is "one of the weightiest and strongest of
his pillars."

The man dies amid tears and is buried
with flowers. His home is sold ; alterations
Walled Up. are made in the house ; the position of a wall of masonry is
changed, and there, walled up in a cavity,
the workmen find the skeleton of a man
murdered and secreted by the dead church
member.

All are not guilty of so notorious and
black a crime, but there are few families and
Skeletons. few individuals who do not have
skeletons which will appear at
Judgment to the woe and disaster of the

guilty. "Secret things shall be revealed." Oh, sinner, confess your sins NOW! Drag your skeletons out of their hiding holes while there is yet opportunity to procure pardon! Jesus will forgive if you "*confess and forsake*" your sins. Better that men talk about us now, and make our ears tingle with embarrassment in the present, than that Eternity be spent amid the hissing of hell's serpents.

Let us stand on the vast plain before God's Judgment throne. There are some fearful sights here. Yonder is a sinner **Awful Sights.** burying his face in his hands and moaning like a dying man. "O hide me from those pure eyes," he shrieks, "the eyes of Him that sitteth upon the throne!"

Strange that this man should be so excited. He has an unblemished reputation. His wife and sons and daughters **"O my God!"** love him tenderly. Why should the Judgment Day arouse his fears? Ask him. He does not hear. Ask him again. His answer is moaned out, "O my God! O my God! O my God!" Put your question

again.   He looks up with the face of a fiend
filled with terror and remorse.   At last he
says: "Oh, sir," and the words are wrung
from him like teeth from the jaw ; "Oh sir,
men call me good ! Ha, ha ! " (This laughter chills the blood of the hearer.)   "What
a lie !   I am not good.   I am black as the
bottomless Pit.   Why, sir, *I am the father of
an unowned, bastard son.*"

"The world does not know that I am base.
My wife does not know it.   I kept the thing
"In the   hushed up. My family could never
Toils."   have raised their heads again if the
matter had been known, but now, O God,
God, God ! help me ! help me ! I am in the
toils of judgment, and the revelation of all
things is at hand. "

Yes, the revelation will come, and this
man's sad plight will be that of many a poor
Many a   soul.   What startling disclosures
Poor Soul   will be made !   What dreadful
facts will come to light !   What strange
mysteries will be explained !

Christ will sit on His throne before teem-
ing millions of souls, each individual, if

guilty, wincing and cringing beneath the red-hot needle of His piercing gaze. The face that attracted the children was the same face that looked on Peter and melted his heart so that "he went out and wept bitterly," and the same face will fill the impenitent with horror and fear, and cause them to cry out to rocks and mountains to fall on them.

The Face of Christ.

Who will be present? All the murderers that the world has ever seen will be there for judgment and sentence. Pomeroy says, in one of his sermons: "There will be there all the great man-monsters who have reveled in carnage and waded ankle-deep in blood. The iron-hearted Pharaoh, the king slave-driver of olden times; the cruel Herod; Xerxes, that world in arms who convulsed the Roman Empire and stripped three bushels of golden rings from her slaughtered lords; Alexander, who drove his wheels hub-deep in blood and begirt the globe with the track of ruin; Cæsar, who laid in waste eight hundred cities and mur-

Who Will Be There?

dered a million of his brethren; Bonaparte, who filled the world with the terror of his name, and deluged Europe in tears—all will be there, but not now to awe down ranks and armies, but there in sad dismay.

"Infidels will be there with the revilers of Christ and His religion, and all that race of Scoff and Blasphemy. God-haters who make bywords of Jehovah's titles, gloating over the sacred names of Him who died for them, speaking "Christ" and "Jesus" with a demon greed, smacking satisfaction from scoff and blasphemy.

"Backsliders will be there to see Him who once forgave all their sins— Backsliders. to whom they once did pray, of whom they sang and talked."

What regrets will fill the heart of the back-slider! How sadness will cover him like Past Opportunities. a cloud when he remembers his slighted and neglected opportunities. The same eminent preacher quoted above, addressing backsliders, says: "You have trod under foot your Savior, and counted the blood of the covenant wherewith you were sanctified an unholy thing, and 'done despite to the spirit of grace.' I look a little forward, and, behold, you are at the Judgment. Yes, you are there in murderous blood—the mark is on you—it is on your feet. How hard you trod Him down when you treated with contempt His salvation! Oh, how drabbled in Atonement blood you are!

"As these blood-spotted multitudes are made to face retribution, I seem to see restrained lightning grow restless Blood-Spotted Multitudes. and fiery. Oh, how its forkedness shoots out like adders' tongues—lurid and red, all tremulous with charged damnations, as if in haste to be avenged on that spotted throng. How Atonement blood on feet stirs the vials of *wrath*. But they are there aghast.

"Though *here* they may not only deny Christ, but deny their conversion also, and glory in the concealment of former The Mark is on Thee. days when they prayed and praised, swearing it all a lie; but the mark is on thee, O backslider! And though thou mightest mix with common sinners and heathens vast, and think to pass for one of them, yet the rankling arrows in Jehovah's quiver would give signs of the approach of spotted feet in that crowd.

"Wrath holds a steady aim on thee, O backslider. Now, my brother man, come *The Crash is* back to Him whom you know, *Coming.* whom you have proved to be Jesus. Ask Him to take you in! Come under shelter! Hide away in the clefts of the rock before the storm day comes! For the crash of its coming is already heard! The dark portent gets darker and nearer! O, my friend, get out of these THUNDER ROADS! I say, GET OUT, QUICK! For you are approaching God on the challenge side, where He is a consuming fire. No one going this way ever returned. Do not stay here! You *attract lightning and wrath!* The very thunders rock at sight of thee! Going to Judgment with bloody feet, fresh from the treadings on Jesus Christ, puts all the enginery of ruin astir as if impatient of the sentence, 'DEPART.' "

Another class will be present to their infinite confusion and dismay. The people who have had great light and rejected it will fare hardly at the Judgment. "I had rather," says Henry Clay Morrison, Responsibility of Light. "go up to Judgment from the jungles of Africa, with the bone of a missionary in my hand than from a holiness camp or a full salvation convention, having rejected the light of truth." We are responsible for all the light God gives us, and he who sits obdurate and stiff-necked under a Holy Ghost ministry will reap a damnation fearful in proportion to the inexcusableness of his course. May God help you and me to make ready for the searching scrutiny and severe examinations of that day.

CHAPTER XII.

EXCUSES.

The moment a man sins he begins to cast about for something to excuse his action and The Cause of Excuses. free him from blame. As long as he is right, he *is* right, and feels no need of anything to bolster up his profession of innocence; but when he sins, he feels instinctively that he will be interrogated concerning his act, and therefore fortifies himself with excuses.

An excuse differs from a reason. There is no real reason why a man should play the Excuses not Reasons. fool and neglect Christ's salvation; but the average sinner abounds in excuses, which he is eager to push forward in defense of his course. Sin is unjustifiable and irrational, but every sinner has a pet excuse which *he* esteems positively impregnable.

No sooner did God question Adam than he

94

blamed the woman, and she in turn slan-
dered the Serpent. It is not nat- Shifting the Blame.
ural for depraved human nature
to say frankly, "I am to blame; I am a sinner, inexcusable, willful, and deserving of
hell."

You remember the parable which Christ
related "in the house of one of the chief
Pharisees"—the parable of the The Great Supper.
great supper. That servant who
bade men to the feast was met by some
strange excuses in the course of his round of
calls. All of them were weak, if not absurd.
Like most of the excuses tendered by the impenitent, they were too thin to hide the selfishness that created them.

There was the man who had just bought a
new piece of land, and who "must needs go
see it." Foolish buyer; why did Foolish Buyer.
he buy without knowing the nature
of the property? Why refuse a banquet
without knowing what was to be served?

All over the country men are selling out
their chance of eternal salvation for fields
and farms and books and money and fame

and applause and a thousand and one things that are soon to perish like toad-stools in a scorching sun.

One of the most popular excuses with the unconverted is : *The Christians do not live their religion.* In the first place,

Consistency in Christians. let us say that if you have found no Christians who live their salvation, you have kept poorer company than some of us. It has been granted unto at least a few of us to know those who live consistent, conscientious, Christian lives ; whose desire is God's glory and the good of man ; who

Speak no evil, nay, nor listen to it;

who bear the cares and griefs of life with sweet, patient grace, and bring the light of heaven into this poor, dark world of ours.

And then it is to be doubted whether a sinner is a competent person to judge whether

Not Competent. a man is a real Christian or not. Remember that an unsaved man is an alien, a person without eyes, a creature without spiritual feeling, a soul without life ; and consider whether or no he is the one fitted to judge of the nature of a Christian's life. Like the cow in the fable, who was said to have eaten straw for grass, because her owner put green spectacles over her eyes, the sinner sees everything through the green glasses of his own corrupt nature.

The Word of the Lord says that "to the defiled and unbelieving is nothing pure, but even their own mind and con- A Defiled science is defiled." With a defiled Mind. mind and an unhealthy conscience, how can a sinner judge of the consistency of Christian life? But if we were to grant that all Christians were inconsistent and failed to "live their religion," would that excuse the sinner from doing the best he can? Do other men's inconsistencies excuse him from the duties he owes to God and man?

"*There are too many hypocrites*," shouts an arrogant objector. Indeed! Then why not get converted, and show them Cheats and there can be such a thing as a Shams. genuinely honest man? If there are counterfeits, produce the real gold and put the shams to shame. You say that you "do not want to keep company with hypocrites." All hypocrites are going to hell, and, unless you repent and are converted, you will spend your eternity in the same place. If you would escape the companionship of cheats and pretenders, seek genuine salvation.

The very existence of counterfeits argues the existence of a genuine coin. If there are

Genuine Coin. hypocrites, there must be real Christians, or Satan would not make the spurious money.

Frequently Christian workers are told by those whom they urge to repent, that they "are

An Intentional Liar. good enough," and are "not so very bad," and "are as good as you Christians." Usually the person who makes this speech is a liar, and knows it. We talk of these "moral men who don't need religion!" Most of them are vile as vomit in their hearts, and more deserving of hell than the sot in the saloon. Away with such subterfuge and falsification! God will find thee out yet, thou mouther of black falsehood. Thou mayst whitewash thy tomb as did the Pharisees the tombs of the Fathers, but the rains will destroy the thin profession, the freezing water will crack open thy mausoleum and all the town will see the rotting carcasses.

The man who prides himself on his "honesty" has usually nothing of which to be proud. The "honesty" of the world is a hollow, spectacular affair, with neither body nor bones. It is animated with a desire to *appear* honest. It will make a great parade of itself when its possessor finds a pocket-book, but it will ride in a trolley-car for nothing when the car is crowded and the conductor fails to collect the fare. It will applaud itself for great integrity because it does not keep too much change when a mistake is made in reckoning, but it will oppress in their wages a poor employee, a seamstress, or a servant girl. It is the little thing in the life that indicates the principle of the heart; and if a man will do a dishonest thing that will "never be known," be it ever so "little," he has no principle of honesty.

"I had it once, but lost it," say some in speaking of salvation, *"and I am afraid I can't keep it."* There is hope for

Keep Seeking.

you. The fact that you had it once ought to assure you that its possession is again possible. Your present condition is dangerous, frightfully so. There is no hope for you in your present inactive attitude. Better that you become saved every morning and backslide every night, than that you spend your life hopelessly and inevitably under the sentence of death and condemnation. If you have lost your experience, seek again. Perchance God will take you to heaven during one of your saved periods.

But, oh, friend, there is a better life than this. Surrender completely to the Master,

The "Causing" Power.

trust the cleansing blood implicitly, tell God that the keeping of you is His business, and that you expect Him to do it, walk in all the light that comes, seek and find a clean heart, and you will discover that God has put His Spirit within and is *"causing* you to walk in His statutes."
Praise the Lord!

There are those who say that they *are too bad* to be saved, and that their case is beyond hope. Thanks be unto God that this is not true. God's power is infinite; His grace can not be bounded. He is "able to save to the uttermost ALL that come unto God by him." The only condition is, that you come to God through Jesus, meeting the conditions and trusting His power. It matters not how black your heart, nor how vile your life, the grace of God is fully equal to all your sin.

To the Uttermost-All.

How frequently does Satan secure a soul because it is persuaded that "*there is time enough yet*." Time is such an uncertain thing. No man knoweth what a day will bring forth. Life may not last long for you. You are sure of no time but the present moment. God's time is *NOW*, and for you to put Him off is to run your frail boat into danger.

"Time Enough!"

An unsaved man in an Ohio town had been frequently warned of his danger. He was repeatedly told of the awful peril in which he put his soul by pro-

An Unsaved Man.

crastination. He rejected Christ. He wanted to make a little more money than he had been making, so he prepared his hard cider to sell to the boys at the county fair. Before he had sold a glass his body was a mangled corpse, jammed and jellied by the crush of heavy barrels rolled upon him in a tossing wagon drawn by runaway horses. Play at dice with the devil with your soul at stake, and he will always win, for his dice are loaded.

A flimsy excuse, often made by the awakened sinner, is, *"I shall be made fun of if I* become a Christian."* Oh, thou

Consummate Folly.

cowardly soul, wouldst thou do without eternal, never-ending salvation, because of thy fear of the smile of scorn, the finger pointed in ridicule, the taunting word? What consummate folly! There are but a few years here at most, but beyond the River there is no end to time! Think upon Eternity. Count the cost. What tremendous things hang upon the way thou believest and livest here! Dare opposition, defamation, loss of friends, unpopularity, anything or everything, but do not let Christ turn from the door uninvited to enter.

"*I want to enjoy the world.*" How empty this excuse! You risk your soul for the pleasure of a few moments of sin. An Empty Excuse. How insane is it for us to trade eternal weal for the gilt and tinsel of worldly joys! Pray do not insult your better nature and saner moments.

A very few objectors to present salvation excuse themselves by saying that the Bible is an immoral book. No charge A Boomerang Criticism. could be more false and none could reflect more certainly to the discredit of the morals of the speaker. There are even so-called ministers who find fault with the Holy Scripture on this score. In this connection let me quote the sound words of one of the great preachers of the age:

"Some say there are things in the Bible unfit to be read. Now, I have to say that, if a man is shocked with what he A Prurient Taste. calls the indelicacies of the Word of God, he is prurient in his taste and imagination. If a man can not read the book of

Solomon's Song without impure suggestion, he is either in his heart or in his life a libertine.   The Old Testament description of wickedness, uncleanness of all sorts, is purposely and righteously a disgusting account, instead of the Byronic and the Parisian vernacular, which makes sin attractive instead of appalling.   When those old prophets point you to a lazaretto, it is a lazaretto.

"When a man, having begun to do right, falls back into wickedness and gives up his *Plain Pictures.* integrity, the Bible does not say he was overcome by the fascinations of the festal board, or that he surrendered to convivialities, or that he became a little fast in his habits. I will tell you what the Bible says: 'The dog is turned to his own vomit again, and the sow that was washed to her wallowing in the mire.'   No gilding of iniquity.   No garlands on a death's head.   No pounding away with a silver mallet at iniquity, when it needs an iron sledge hammer.

"I can easily understand how people, brooding over the description of uncleanness

in the Bible, may get morbid in mind, until
they are as full of it as the wings   Carbolic
and the nostril and the claw of   Acid.
a buzzard are full of the odors of a carcass;
but what is wanted is not that the Bible be
disinfected, but that you have your heart and
mind washed with carbolic acid ! I tell you
that a man who does not like this Book, and
who is critical as to its contents, and who is
shocked and outraged with its descriptions,
has never been soundly converted. The lay-
ing on of the hands of presbytery or episco-
pacy does not change a man's heart, and
men sometimes get into the pulpit, as well
as into the pew, never having been changed
radically by the sovereign grace of God.
Get your heart right and the Bible will be
right."

My unsaved friend, there is absolutely no
good excuse for your remaining unsaved.
Your circumstances are no worse than those
of many another soul. At any rate, God
knows your circumstances, and when He
asks you to repent and believe in Jesus He

not only fathoms the depth of your difficulty, but will give you grace to overcome.

Throw away your excuses. They are valueless—worse than nothing. Fall at Jesus' feet, pleading, not your worthiness, but His atonement. Cast yourself entirely on His mercy, and He will blessedly save you.

CHAPTER XIII.

REPENTANCE.

There is nothing which has a more important and necessary place in the plan of salvation than repentance, and yet, Repentance Shunned. strange to say, there is nothing the discussion of which is more scrupulously avoided, and the preaching of which is more generally neglected, than this same theme. This is due to a number of reasons: First, for a man to repent implies a break in the habit of life and mind. Habits are like chains, and hold us with an almost unbreakable power. It is no easy thing for a man to "right about face," and stem the current of his whole past and force himself to a new condition of affairs.

Again, repentance is unwelcome to the sinning individual, because, in Unwelcome. order for a man to repent, he must confess that he is a sinner and in need of salvation. The unregenerate soul is always proud. The absence of anything of which to be proud does not embarrass it in the least. Just to own up "I am a sinner" is one of the hard things a man has to do to repent.

Before a man can truly repent he must be sorry that he sinned—not sorry that he was caught, merely; the man in striped clothes behind iron gratings is all that—but sorry because he has offended the dignity of God's holy government, and inexcusably broken a just and perfect law.

Sorrow for Sin.

Repentance also includes confession of sin. And right here our bark of discussion strikes the end of many a sunken log in our voyage up-stream. "Confession! Confess what?" Confess your sins! What does the clarion-clear Word say? "He that covereth his sins *shall not* prosper, but he that *confesseth* and *forsaketh* shall have mercy!" That is the one safety for the sinner, confession of sin.

Confession.

Unconfessed sins never die. They will ford rivers, and vault mountains, and tra-

verse prairies, and swim oceans, but what
they will find us out, and, like blood-   Bones
hounds in Southern swamps, bury   Within.
their white teeth in our quivering flesh.
You can dupe men, but you can't fool God.
You can make the outside fair and beautiful.
You can be like the hypocrites of Jesus'
day—"whited sepulchers"—but the piercing eye of God sees the grinning jaws and
bare skulls and repulsive joints inside. You
may smile and bow, and appear amiable,
and suave, and respectable, and polite, and
all that, but if there are unconfessed sins in
your life God sees them, and the sleuth-
hound Vengeance will yet put his nose to
your track and dog you to your final damnation!

The fourth point in repentance is the aban-
donment of sin. Our tears and sobs and
groans do not avail, unless we   Quitting Sin.
forsake sin once for all. So long
as we hold on to some hidden uncleanness,
some bosom iniquity, so long Heaven is as
brass to our cries, and our groans do not ac-
complish anything in our behalf.

Frequently one must make restitution before pardon can be obtained. John the Baptist insisted that "fruits" in keeping with a profession of repentance be brought forth. If there are bad debts back in the "years ago" they must be paid. If there has been gossip, and some one's reputation has been injured, that thing must be made right. We can not afford to juggle with infinite justice; we can not afford to wait until the throne is set to find out the worst about ourselves.

Bad Debts.

The caption of this chapter is truly an unpopular one, but it is none the less salutary on that account. Preachers frequently take odd and strange themes in these Dark Ages, but few of them care to be so "peculiar" and "harsh" as to preach frequently on this cardinal doctrine of repentance.

Unpopular Subject.

Repentance is taught in the Bible, if anything is. If the Word of God is to be believed it is "Repent or Perish!" Which will we do? Every man under God's blue vault of heaven has an op-

Repent or Perish!

portunity to repent and make friends with Jesus Christ. How a man treats this opportunity depends wholly upon himself. Just as a motor-man on an electric car by changing the position of the switch determines the direction which the car shall take, so every responsible human being by the choices and volitions of his own heart either sends his soul speedily up the grade to glory or plunging into the abyss of hell!

Will you repent? That is the all-important question. Heaven, and the angels, and good men, and all pure spirits en- "Will You treat you to repent; devils, and de- Repent?" mons, and black imps, and mockers of the Son of God hold you back in impenitence. ¡ *Break from the chains and irons of Satan's power! You have a choice between eternal light and never-ceasing blackness, between wondrous redemption and direst damnation!*

There is not a sad-faced, smoke-grimed soul in the Pit that would not advise you to repent. Dives in the torments of Dives' Wish. the dark regions of despair pleads that Father Abraham will send the former

beggar Lazarus to his five impenitent brethren lest they come into that place of woe.
That is the sentiment of all those poor souls
who drop into hell. So far from desiring
companionship they seek to hinder the unsaved from coming.

We sometimes hear rash persons say, "If
my husband or wife, or friend, or loved one,"
A Rash
Speech. as the case may be, "is going to
hell, then I want to go with them."
But, friend, they would not want you. They
would abhor your presence. You would be
a constant, aggravating reminder of their
folly in refusing proffered salvation. They
would blame themselves for your catastro-
phe, and writhe beneath the unconscious re-
proach of your sad eyes.

Genuine repentance is a rare thing. As
the late Laureate wrote :

> "This world will not believe a man repents,
>   And this wise world of ours is mainly right;
>   And seldom does a man repent and use
>   Both grace and will to pick the vicious quick
>   Of blood and custom wholly out of him,
>   And make all new and plant himself afresh."

It is so easy for a man to suppose that he has repented when he is many leagues from it. Satan is in the counterfeiting business on a large scale. He manufactures an infinite number of spurious repentances, and palms them off on awakened sinners, persons who are really alarmed about their condition, but who dread the stern, inexorable principles of Scriptural penitence. **Duped Sinners.**

Fright is often mistaken for evangelical repentance. The infidel who bellows to God in a storm at sea, making vows of future piety, is not penitent; he is simply scared. The number of death-bed professions of repentance which are genuine are very, very few. This is proven by careful observation of those who, supposing that they are to die, unexpectedly recover. Usually the pretension of penitence is entirely disregarded, and the life of sin is resumed at the point where sickness interfered. **Fright Not Repentance.**

Let us remember that, however good our experience may seem to be, if there are wrong things not made right to the best of our ability, we have not truly **Covered Sins.**

repented. If there are thefts unconfessed, if there are bastards unowned, if there are lies covered over, if there are bills unpaid, and we are patting ourselves on the shoulder and calling ourselves Christians, we are deceived, and the devil will surely get us if we do not alter our course.

If there were more genuine cases of repentance there would be more Scriptural conversions and more examples of old-time shouting and more cases of the conscious witness of the Spirit than we see to-day. A house is no safer than its foundation is solid, and a man's experience is no more secure than the thoroughness of his first beginning in the spiritual life.

A Good Foundation.

Let us take heed to our repentance, for it is the initial work. It is man's first step toward the Cross. Let us make no mistake here. We can not afford to err or deceive ourselves in a matter so important. Determine first of all to get right at all costs. Pray God to ferret out all the intricacies of your sin. Take sides against sin at every turn. Leave sin so de-

"Let Us Take Heed."

cidedly as to die rather than go back to it. Only by this thorough route can you hope for mercy at God's hands.

But it will do no good to "turn from sin" unless we also "turn to God." We must find a Friend as powerful as was the grip of sin, otherwise we will Turning to God. again feel the steel fingers throttling our throats. *Jesus is our only hope. To Him let us all turn, for He will turn to us and speak pardon and peace.*

CHAPTER XIV.

CONVERSION—BECOMING A CHRISTIAN.

"Ye must be born again," said the Master Teacher to His midnight visitor, and this is

Christless Morality.

His solemn message to every sinning soul. We are living in the times of the Decadence, so far as faith in and possession of deep Christian experiences is concerned. A Christless, bloodless morality is lauded to the firmament; a conscious, vital soul-experience of holy things is looked upon askance.

We are much interested of late, it seems, in brilliant schemes for improving tenement

Leaving Jesus Out.

life and adjusting the conflict between capital and labor, but we do not preach Christ and Him crucified with the fervor nor with the success of our fathers. We are sanguine and expectant concerning "the Keely cure" and the Elmira Reformatory, but our plan leaves Jesus out and takes no account of a real change of heart.

Take a criminal, if you like, and feed him on "choice, selected vegetables," give him "cereals" and "not too much meat," "exercise" him regularly, *A Rotten Heart.* and "be sure that his room is well ventilated," improve his health and strengthen his muscles; but think not to make a bad heart good, an Isaac out of an Ishmael, a Paul out of a Nero, a Saint Jerry MacAuley out of a villain from the dives of Water Street. A rotten heart is ever a rotten heart until GOD undertakes its alteration. *There is absolutely no hope but in the new birth.*

Conversion must be something more than mere reformation. The world has great confidence in the latter for the reason *The World's Kind.* that the man who reforms his life "pays up his bills." The world is always glad to have its bills paid, and is, of course, in favor of a "conversion" that means money in pocket for it; but the conversion of the Bible, the conversion wrought in the heart by the Holy Ghost, that which not only hews

off the limbs of a tree, but digs for the root;
which not only mows the front lawn, but
cleans up the old boots, decaying vegetables,
and sardine cans of the back yard; that
which makes a man's invisible life as correct
as that which appears, is in direct antagon-
ism to the creed of the world, and calls forth
its venom and virulence.

Yes, Bible conversion is more than reformation. Supposing that a man *does* stop
A Different   drink, his pent-up current of sin-
Cloak.   fulness in the unregenerated heart
will only manifest itself in greater lechery
or increased profanity or some other devilish
role. The "reformed man," who is unregenerated, is usually so proud of his whitewash that there is no living with him peace-
ably. His conversation is one monotonous
strain of boast and brag. The devil of drink
has changed his cloak and bobbed up again a
devil of pride.

Reformation is a human work, and, there-
The Apothe-   fore, without avail in combating
osis of Man.   the grim dragon—*Sin.* We are
living in a day when what man does is "the

glory of the age." Man's "culture," "colleges," "inventions," "philosophies," "oratory," "criticism," "warfare," these are the little gods of civilization, and God is draped in white cloths and set aside in some out-of-the-way corner. But unless GOD *saves* us by a divine power, unless He steps in and does what man can no more do than he can make a world, all men must sink in death, struck by the red-hot thunderbolts wielded by incensed Justice.

The potency of the work in the heart called conversion lies in the fact of a new birth. We are more than adopted, A Noble Heritage. we are born from above and become "partakers of the divine nature." We are not only heirs of heaven, but heirs of divine traits and characteristics. The grandest inheritance a child can receive from its parent is not a farm, nor a railroad, nor a steamship, but a tender conscience, a love of nobleness, a delicate taste, a fondness for books, a leaning toward piety and simplicity. God's sons inherit the divine attitude and taste so that sin and salvation, meanness and spiritual-mindedness, selfishness and generosity of soul are looked upon in the same way.

So wonderful is the transformation wrought in a man at his heavenly birth, regeneration, "All Things New." that the entire world assumes a new face and a fresh meaning. Old things are passed away, and behold all things are become new. "When I walked from the old church to my home the very leaves seemed to exult and praise God, while the tiny birds sang, Peace, Peace," said a creditable testifier in a convention, speaking of his conversion.

This marvelous work, colossal though it is, does not depend upon length of days for Instantaneous. its completion. A birthday is not a series of years, but a specific day. A ball rolling down hill, stopped by an agile boy, and sent spinning back again, has a specific, definite instant in its history when it began to retrace its course. A sinner plunging down the precipitous path toward the Eternal Ditch, does not begin to go the other way by a gradual process.

There is an instant when he begins to move up the mountain, down the steep side of which he was but an instant before rushing recklessly.

The fact that salvation is by faith proves it to be an instantaneous work. Since it is by faith, it is not of man, for faith is only man depending on God to do what he himself can not do. God does not pardon gradually. That is not His nature. The "gradualists" are ever incomplete and unsatisfied in their assurance of salvation. Faith must reach a point where we can trust God to pardon ALL our sins, and do it NOW.

By Faith.

From the time the soul is born anew it possesses overcoming power and will possess it as long as confidence in God abides and fidelity to His Word remains. The man who is not an overcomer is overcome. We must either with St. Michael stand victorious on the Dragon, Sin, or with Judas Iscariot feel the sharp claws of his merciless feet. Is your life an overcoming life? If not, examine your experi-

St. Michael.

ence carefully and learn whether you are a real Christian or not.

God in His mercy has provided power for us to overcome temptation at every point.

Iron Wheels.   If you are being ground beneath the iron wheels of the car of Juggernaut, it is because you are not in possession of the conquering principle which a genuine conversion always brings into the heart.

When we are converted we receive the graces of the Spirit—love, joy, peace, patience, longsuffering, etc.,—and The Spirit-Graces.   while they are not perfected and given full sway in the heart until entire sanctification, yet their presence is an inexpressible boon to the convert. "Of His fulness have all we received and grace for grace"; that is to say, for every beauteous grace in Jesus there is a corresponding miniature in the breast of a real Christian.

How simple is the way of salvation. Its The Simple Way.   very simplicity repels the profound and those who think to philosophize themselves into heaven.

Be sure, O seeking one, that you are sin-
cere from crown to toe. Toy not with the
arrows of Omnipotence, dance not   Honesty and
on the buckler of God. If you   Earnestness.
are honest throughout, there is hope. To
your honesty add earnestness. "When ye
seek *with your whole heart* ye shall find me,"
says the Lord.

Honestly and earnestly *yield yourself to
Jesus now.* Having repented, and I trust
that every reader has performed
that duty ere this chapter was   Trust.
read, there is nought to do but *surrender absolutely* to God and *trust the blood to cover all
your sins.*

Be sure that you trust Him now. Look
not to feeling for salvation. Do not expect
to feel until there is first a fact to   Fact and
cause feeling. The first great mis-   Feeling.
take seekers are apt to make is to fail to
surrender, and the second is to expect and
wait for *feeling*, instead of believing that
just now, according to the promise of God,
the Atonement does cancel all the sins of
the past life. Bring your faith-faculty to

the active pitch.   Say with the hymn-
writer :

> "The cross *now* covers my sins,
> The past *is* under the blood,
> I *am trusting* in Jesus for all,
> My will *is* the will of my God."

Having taken God at His word, and believed that He "in no wise casts you out,"
The Witness but rather takes you in, there is
of the Spirit. nought to do, but confidently and
expectantly await the coming of the witness
of the Spirit.   If your surrender is perfect
and your faith is complete, God will perform
the work and *tell you that it is done.*   The
"telling you that it is done" is the witness.
It is a sweet, calm, restful peace that steals
over the troubled waters of the soul whis-
pering, "It is done ! It is done ! My sins
are pardoned.   I am a child of God."

CHAPTER XV.

SOME CHARACTERISTICS OF REAL CHRISTIANS.

Salvation does not consist in works, nor in the absence of them. It is of grace, the "free, unmerited gift" of a generous and compassionate God. And **By their Fruits.** yet "by their fruits shall ye know them." If an experience is genuine, its genuineness is attested by visible works. A "faith" that is "without works" is a "dead," valueless faith. James saw the danger that so many run into, that of trusting in faith only and entirely disregarding the necessity of good works. Therefore did he utter his startling sentence, a warning to all, lest religion become a thing of theory and not fact, a matter of talk and not practice.

In the first place, let us remember that if a man is a child of God he does not break the known law of God, i. e., he does not sin.

He that sins is a sinner, and no Christian.
John says a Christian *can not* sin,
Sinning.
and at the same time be a child
of God. Whoever heard of a thieving honest
man, a pure libertine, or a conscientious
knave? Neither is their such a thing as a
sinning Christian.

"But the Westminster Con"—. Very
true, but the BIBLE says, "He that is born of
God doth not commit sin." The
Westminster Confession.
Bible will stand when "creeds"
and "confessions" are mildew and ashes.
"But I sin in word, thought and deed every
day." Indeed, so does the devil! Would
you know your pedigree? Then turn again
to John: "*He that committeth sin is of the
devil.*" He who boasts of his sinning is like
the leper who boasts of his sores or the har-
lot who glories in her shame.

There is among others a very blessed
promise in the New Testament preceded
by a very stern command. The
Blessed Promises.
promise is given by God, and He
says that, after certain things have been
done, He "will receive us, and will be a

Father unto us, and we shall be his sons and daughters." What precious words! To be received by the King of Heaven, to have Him for our Father, and to live in the consciousness of sonship, what could be more blessed than privileges like these?

But mark! God's promises and His commands go hand in hand, and, *unless the latter are obeyed, the benefits of the former* **Stern Commands.** *can not be enjoyed.* What are the commands in connection with these gracious promises (II. Cor. vi. 14)? *"Be ye not unequally yoked together with unbelievers. . . . What concord has Christ with Belial? or what part hath he that believeth with an infidel? . . . Wherefore come out from among them and be ye separate, saith the Lord, and touch not the unclean thing."*

These words are followed by the glorious promises previously quoted. But what strong words are these! Evidently, if **Separation.** God is going to receive us and take us into His family, we must separate ourselves in a very important sense from the world. While we are compelled to associate in business or work with the world, yet we *simply can not affiliate with sinners in their Christless pleasures and practices* AND REMAIN *Christians.*

Supposing that it were possible to convict an organization of the crime of murder. That

The Murder
of Morgan.

is, suppose that it could be shown that, according to the direction of the officers and with the sworn consent of its members, a man was foully dealt with and sent to death. Could a follower of Jesus Christ belong to this organization and remain innocent? Would not his hands be red with the blood of a dead man?

Those who have taken the pains to know are fully aware that the vile, sneaking mur-

Free-
Masonry.

der of Morgan was committed by the Masons. *To that institution, Free-Masonry, is chargeable this unjustifiable crime.* If you are a Mason, and do not know this, do not show your ignorance by denying that the deed was done. Moreover, you are under oath to agree to consent to and aid in the detection and punishment even to death itself of all Masons who divulge the silly secrets of the fraternity. *You are promised to murder, if so directed by your superiors in the organization, so long as you remain a Mason.* And yet you say that you are a disciple of Jesus Christ, who said, "In secret have I said nothing." Away with such hypocritical pretension!

"But they do lots of good." Yes, indeed, and we all hear of it when it is done. It is trumpeted and magnified far and wide. An orange for a sick man, **Empty Work.** a big parade when he is dead, several million dollars in fine temples, and plenty of costly banquets—are these your "good works"?

"If a man is a good Mason, he is a Christian." It is a lie, and comes from the pit smelling of sulphur. *Did you* **Christless** *ever hear the "Chaplain" honor* **Lodges.** *Christ in the lodge?* Let him pray to Jesus if he wants to, but the chances are that he will be hissed. The Masons claim to honor God the Father, but "he that hath not the Son hath not the Father," saith the Word.

A man may be a good secret order man and be an infidel, an agnostic, atheist, almost anything but a Christian. We have spoken

Jesus
Slighted.

of the Masons because they are
representative ; what is true of
of them is *in general* true of all secret orders.
Christ is ignored, and the blood is dishon-
ored, and the church of Jesus antagonized.

The man who undertakes to maintain connection with these Christless organizations,

An Opened
Artery.

whether by attending the meetings
or merely paying his "dues," is
like a man who opens an artery to see the
blood run. He may think he is progressing
in things spiritual, but his friends can see
all too plainly that he is weak compared with
what he would be if he *obeyed God* and
"came out from among them and was separate and touched not the unclean thing."

When Judgment comes I do not want my
feet tangled in a net of godless connections

Nets.

and hindrances, do you? Let us
cut loose from all but God and
salvation and grow strong in the things of
the Lord.

So the real Christian has no use for secret
orders. He has nothing to hide. Like his

Master, he is open and transparent. Are you a real Christian?

Another thing which the real Christian does not do, is mix with giddy worldlings in whist and euchre parties. You will find plenty of church members at these gatherings, but they are not God's children. Extenuate these "society events" as we may, they are first cousins to the gambling den, and are as much accursed in the sight of God. "Play cards in your own home," if you choose, but do not blame "fate," or "fortune," or God if your son is a gambler.

Whist and Euchre.

The genuine Christian pays his debts. Of course, there are cases where a man simply can not get out of debt. Such a man God excuses until he can pay. He may live very close to God and be in an unavoidable debt; but if a man *can* pay his bills he either pays them or else is not a real Christian. "Owe no man anything but love," is the Bible principle, and it is the only safe and consistent one for followers of the Nazerene.

Debt Paying.

The idea of church members having bills stand for years unthought of and unheeded!

Robbing Creditors. There are men who talk long and loud in meeting who make no effort to pay, and yet in their homes there are plenty of silverware, and china, and food sufficient to stuff the stomach three times a day! Do not "give your debts to the Lord" in the sense of not making persistent, wise, whole-hearted efforts to pay them.

The New Testament Christian so constantly walks with God and so **Church Fairs.** continually lives in prayer and His presence, that he gets to look at things the way his Companion looks at them. The matter of gospel finance is regarded by him in a Pentecostal light. God's plan is that the church should be supported by the free-will offerings of the people. Backsliders forsake God in this His method, and resort to worldly "suppers," "fairs," "bazaars," "festivals," and "parties" to support the work of the great God!

If a man is converted at all he will give gladly without being made to pay a quarter for a fifteen-cent lunch.   It is the worldling and the man who has drifted "The Supper Crowd." from God who find their element in the church supper crowd.   The *salvation man*, the man who really knows Jesus, has something better to do than give money through worldly channels, or aid in planning and running ecclesiastical restaurants and theaters.   May the illuminating Spirit enable us to see whether we are professors merely, or possessors of the grace of Jesus Christ.

God plants in the breast of every child of which He is the spiritual Father a hatred of indelicate situations and gatherings.   If you are seeking a true A Holy Taste. Christian, you will be more likely to find him in his house at prayer than at the grocery spinning dirty "yarns" or listening to some other spinner.   The claws and beak of the buzzard smell of carrion; the prayers of the saints are like "incense, acceptable to God." A man goes where his tastes carry him.   We all go to "our own company."   Religion is a "matter of taste."   If we have a taste for ribaldry, gossip, filth, garbage, we will naturally gravitate toward them ; if our taste is holy, we will delight in prayer, in God's Word, in clean, edifying conversation.

Nowhere does a man's taste more unmistakably declare him than when we come to the tobacco question. "Can a man be a Christian and use tobacco?" said a questioner to the great Chicago evangelist. The great head dropped a moment, and he replied, "Perhaps, but he would be a nasty one." Light has come in greater strength since those words were spoken, and there is doubt now whether a man can be a Christian at all and use the poisonous nicotine. These repulsive creatures that infest the three back seats of an open trolley car, these whom the railroad companies compel to ride in a coach by themselves because of their obnoxious habit, can it be that they are faithful followers of the Christ of the seamless robe, the fair, holy Lily of the Judean valley? No wonder that thoughtful men doubt that such a thing is possible.

Tobacco Worms.

The Bible declares against "all filthiness of the flesh and spirit." Tobacco is an unclean habit, and if you are a genuine Christian you want cleanliness, not filth.

"All Filthiness."

Christ's followers are Bible Christians. The Bible is their guide, their law, their check-book, their rule of faith and practice. When pardon comes, love for the Bible comes with it, and to the justified man the Book of books has ever a constant and alluring power.

Bible Christians.

If we are truly converted we will show our experience by faithfulness in little things as well as in greater. Kindness of manner, sympathy for the afflicted and the poor and unfortunate, courtesy toward a common washerwoman as genuine as that to the princess, carefulness to speak the truth and refrain from uncharitableness in speaking of others, chastity of thought and imagination, these and swarms of other little things are the indices to our experience.

Little Things.

May God help us to ask ourselves the

searching question, "Am I a true child of
God?" If we are not, let us waste
no time, but "do the first works,"
submit to Jesus, trust His grace and really
become that which we have before merely
professed to be.

CHAPTER XVI

INSTRUCTIONS TO CONVERTS.

After we have given our all to Jesus, we may rest assured that He will give us a perfect pardon, a complete and nor- The Rapidity mal birth into the family of God of Progress. by the power of the Spirit. While all converts are equally fortunate in birthright and family privileges, not all make the same progress after conversion. The rapidity of progress depends upon the nearness with which we follow the plan of God for us as revealed in the Word.

There is one thing the young convert must not neglect, and that is his Bible. It is " God's love letter " to the church, God's Love and deserves the most careful and Letter. persevering study. Pore over it upon your knees. Search the Scriptures. Commit choice promises to memory. Equip yourself with the panoply to be found in this celestial armory.   Remember that when Satan attacked Jesus, our Master replied at each assault, "It is written," and well for us if our familiarity with God's Book enables us to repel the same enemy in the same way.

A lawyer must know his law books if he is to win cases, a physician must familiarize himself with his medical authorities if he is to cure patients, and **Delving Deep.** the Christian must delve deep in his Bible if he is to succeed at *his* business, that of living for God and souls.

The man who makes rapid strides in divine things must frequently visit the closet of secret prayer.   We should, of **Secret Prayer.** course, have the spirit of prayer, but the spirit of prayer will continue only by our maintaining regular, stated seasons of prayer.   Regular prayer increases the spirit of prayer, and the spirit of prayer gives life to the regular season of devotion.   The two act reflexly and help each other.

Talk things over with God.   While godly men and women can frequently give you wholesome advice, yet God has reserved

for Himself the privilege of talking to the
soul first hand, solving problems, **God Our Portion.**
clearing mists, stamping rainbows
on dark clouds, and making the heart conscious of divine comfort. Happy the Christian who learns early in his career that there
is no consolation to be found in man. Make
up your mind to bury your griefs in the
bosom of Jesus and give sunshine to others. God is our comfort, our portion, our
companion, our blessing; to Him turn always when in need rather than to the dry
springs of human words.

Remember that *salvation is by faith*, *not
feeling*. Feeling comes with it, but it is a
side-dish, not essential at all times. **Press On.**
If some morning your spring of
exuberance is not so geyser-like as the night
you were converted, do not conclude that you
are fallen from grace; perhaps you only have
a little indigestion. Emotions frequently
depend on causes purely physical. If you
are all the Lord's and trusting the blood and
are not conscious of having committed sin,
do not side with the devil and be cast down.

Raise a shout of triumph. Tell Satan to go to Jesus your Redeemer with his accusations, and press on undismayed toward the shining City.

If by some evil chance you fall into sin, do not lie in the mud an instant. Run to "If You Fall." Jesus! Confess your fall! Plead the blood! Believe the promise as at first! He who commanded His disciples to forgive a sinning brother four hundred and ninety times in one day will not turn away from you after your tumble, provided your penitence is genuine.

The only way to be sure of keeping power and constant victory is to walk with and Obeying the Spirit. obey the Holy Spirit. While the newly converted man can not properly be said to be BAPTIZED *with the Holy Ghost* until he experiences the work of entire sanctification, yet *he has the Holy Spirit with him*, and may rest assured of His co-operation and encouragement. In entire sanctification the Spirit comes into the heart, cleansing it, and giving Himself in His fulness. But, even in the merely justified experience,

He is constantly visiting the soul, cheering the heart and protecting it from sin.

The young Christian must make up his mind from the first that he will, by the grace of God, bear faithful testimony for his Lord and Master. To fail ***Bearing Testimony.*** at this point is to be a Major Andre, a Benedict Arnold, a traitor to the cause of Jesus Christ. Whenever opportunity is given, bear testimony to the saving power of the blood of your Savior. Do not preach yourself, but Jesus. Do not brag of your past sinfulness, but modestly, truthfully, explicitly relate what God has done for your soul.

When you are in the presence of sinners, "let your light shine." If you are ashamed before men, the great Christ will ***Letting Light Shine.*** blush to own you at the Last Day. Do not let a man soil, with his foul lips, the name of the Lord who died for you, without being rebuked for his wickedness. If a man tells a smutty joke in your presence, do not laugh, but rather rebuke him. Deal thus faithfully with sinners and your heart will at length be gladdened by the fruit that shall result.

Attend upon the means of grace. Do not allow Satan to magnify business in your
The Means
of Grace. eyes until you omit the prayer-meeting or think you can not push things aside and get to a camp-meeting or a convention, or some other means of grace which has ever proved a glorious blessing to the people of God. Assemble with God's people. With David rejoice when it is possible to "go unto the house of the Lord." Hearken carefully to the message preached by God's ministers in so far as they follow Christ. At all times, by all means, seek to know the truth, grow in grace and increase in the knowledge of God.

No Christian can afford to be idle. "An idle mind is the devil's workshop," said
Be Active. Martin Luther, and the truth of the epigram is seen in the wrecks all about us. This is a devilish world, and you have wasted too much time in sin to be able to afford indolence now. There is a Bible to read, there are requests to make at

the Throne, there are souls to save. If you have work or business, apply yourself industriously, not for "filthy lucre," or worldly wealth, but that you may have wherewithal to help on the work of the Lord. "Diligent in business, fervent in spirit, serving the Lord."

Let us remark right here that there is much blessing and profit to be found by young Christians, as well as those more advanced, by giving at least *Giving a Tenth.* a tenth of your gross income to God. If the church of America did this much, there would be sufficient funds to support a minister to every seventeen Christians. There is no call for so many pastors, but the money is certainly needed in the work of God in foreign fields.

The old Jew gave a tenth, and shall the Christian, who is not under law, but thanks be to God, under grace, do less? *Jews and Christians.* Have we not as much cause to show our gratitude by giving as had the Hebrew?

"Yes, but I give more than a tenth." Do

you keep a careful account and see? A

A Big
Quarter.
quarter given in a collection seems bigger than the dollar paid for anything for ourselves. There are few who really give a tenth who do not take accurate care in calculating it.

After the tenth is given, which was the "rent" of Canaan, one can go on in liberal-

Stingy
Professors.
ity as far as one feels inclined. One thing is sure, the men who give too much are rare, while the stingy professors are thick as gnats in June.

"God loveth a cheerful giver." Gordon says that "cheerful" is better rendered

Almoners.
"hilarious." Hilarious givers! What a blessing they are to the world! We meet them now and then, and they are like embassadors from God, almoners of heaven, dispensers of grace and goodness.

There is one thing which the converted man must not by any means fail to do. He

Seek
Holiness.
must seek and find the experience of entire sanctification. The Bible tells us that it "is the will of God" (I.

Thess. iv. 3), and if so, no child of God can refuse it and remain blameless. It is not the purpose of this book to discuss the experience of sanctification, but we can not bid our readers farewell without telling them that the precious, victorious grace of purity wrought in the heart by the baptism with the Holy Ghost *is for all of God's children.* God is no respecter of persons, and what He has done for millions of His followers He will do for you.

"When will He do this?" God's time is NOW. "How can I secure this blessing?" *First.* Consecrate your entire being with all its ransomed powers, **Consecration.** talents, faculties, and members to God. As a sinner you could not consecrate, you could only surrender, "ground arms" as a rebel. Now you have certain powers as a result of redemption, and these you ought to put at God's complete disposal. Say to God with all the earnestness of your soul: "I am willing—

To receive what *Thou* givest,

To lack what *Thou* withholdest,

> To relinquish what *Thou* takest,
> To suffer what *Thou* inflictest,
> To be what *Thou* requirest,
> To do what *Thou* commandest.''

Second. Consecration, however, is not sanctification in the sense we now mean, the sense of John xvii. 17. Consecration is *man's* work; sanctification

Believing.

is *God's* work. So after we are entirely consecrated, the next thing to do is to *trust the blood just now to cleanse from all indwelling sin.* Believe *now* that the altar—Christ—sanctifies the gift—yourself. God is true, though feelings may lie. His promises are good: "Faithful is he that calleth you who also will do it" (II. Thess. v. 24). Do what? "Sanctify you wholly" (v. 23). Yes, praise the Lord, the experience is for us all if we will but consecrate and believe.

God never fails to cleanse the heart of the consecrated, *trusting* man; neither

The Witness.

does He fail to attest His work by a clear, indubitable testimony to the fact.

How plainly does the writer remember his own experience in regard to this wonderful gift of God. In utter helplessness he abandoned himself to the Lord, to be His property forever. Then

Experience.

when at the end of his own resources there was no one else to trust but Jesus, and to Him the arms of his soul stretched out in pleading prayer. He was told to "believe that the blood cleansed." He did so. Almost immediately a sweet, ineffable peace filled his heart, and he knew beyond a doubt that he was sanctified wholly. Praise the Lord.

This sunshiney Canaan-life is God's thought for us all. Shall we come short of His plan and grieve His tender

With Jesus.

heart. Rather let us put our hands confidently in the hands of our Joshua —Jesus, and with Him cleave the rolling Jordan, and with Him possess the fair land of full salvation!

THE END.

Books by Byron J. Rees.

THE HEART CRY OF JESUS.

CLOTH, 40 CENTS.

HULDAH, THE PENTECOSTAL PROPHETESS.

Every sentence is compact and precious as beaten gold.—*The American Friend.*

CLOTH, 50 CENTS.

CHRISTLIKENESS AND OTHER PAPERS.

There is something in it for every one. If you want an uplifting and inspiration for a higher life, read this book.—*Christian Standard.*

PAPER, 25 CENTS.

The Set, Post-paid, $1.00.

WITH

The Weekly Revivalist, $1.80.

Address

M. W. KNAPP,

OFFICE OF THE REVIVALIST,

Cincinnati, O.   Providence, R. I.

Burning Books

By Seth C. Rees,

The Quaker Author and Evangelist.

I. FIRE FROM HEAVEN.

Over 300 pages. Price, $1.00. If you appreciate celestial light and fire, you will be delighted with this book. Four copies, postpaid, for the price of three.

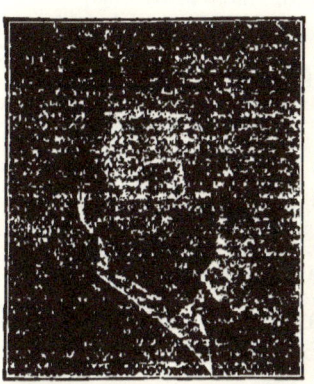

CONTENTS: Chapter I., Fire from Heaven; II., Established in Christ; III., God's Choice of Instruments; IV., Stephen's Fulness; V., The True Saint; VI., Rooted and Grounded; VII., Abounding Grace; VIII., The Secret of the Lord; IX., Exploits; X., A Larger Outlook; XI., Abundant Resources; XII., More Than Conquerors; XIII., This is That; XIV., The Holy Peace; XV., Call of Rebecca; XVI., Blessings in Disguise.

II. PENTECOSTAL CHURCH.

Like the Bible and the Life of Jesus, it combines the characteristics of the Lamb and the Lion, the Lily and the Lightning.

CONTENTS: Chapter I., Opening Words; II., The Ideal Pentecostal Church is Composed of Regenerated Souls; III., A Clean Church; IV., A Powerful Church; V., A Powerful Church—Continued; VI., A Witnessing Church; VII., Without Distinction as to Sex; VIII., A Liberal Church; IX., A Demonstrative Church; X., An Attractive Church—Draws the People Together; XI., Puts People Under Conviction; XII., Will Have Healthy Converts; XIII., A Joyful Church; XIV., A Unit; XV., The Power of the Lord is Present to Heal the Sick; XVI., A Missionary Church; XVII., Out of Bondage; XVIII., Entering into Canaan; XIX., The Land and Its Resources; XX., Samson; XXI., Power Above the Power of the Enemy; XXII., Compromise and Its Evil Effects; XXIII., Sermon; XXIV., The Author's Experience.

Price, 50 cents; four copies, postpaid, $1.50. Special rates by the quantity.

GODBEY'S NEW TESTAMENT COMMENTARY.

VOL. I. Revelation......................Price, **$1.00**
VOL. II. Hebrews (Perfection), James (Practice), Peter (Fire), John (Love), Jude (Lightning). 434 pages. Price, postpaid.............................. **1.25**
VOL. III. Ephesians, Philippians, Colossians, I. and II. Thessalonians, I. and II. Timothy, Titus, and Philemon. Present Price....................... **1.00**
VOL. IV. Corinthians to Galatians. Over 500 pages. Price..................... **1.50**
VOL. V. Acts and Romans, over 500 pages. Price............................ **1.50**

20 per cent. discount to all who order the whole set, paying for each Volume as issued.

NOTICE.

1. It is condensed. It omits all passages which need no explaining, and deals thoroughly with the difficult ones, thus giving the reader the greatest possible value for his money. 2. It throws floods of new light upon many important passages. 3. It shows the proper translation of the New Testament, and sweeps sophistical arguments against holiness triumphantly from the field. 4. It will doubtless be the great Holiness Commentary on the New Testament for coming years, as it is written from a holiness standpoint by one of the ablest evangelistic Greek New Testament translators of any age.

THE GENERAL VERDICT

Of many of its readers is voiced in the following notices of Vol. I.: "Of intense interest."—*The Methodist.* "Practical, spiritual, interesting and instructive."—*Religious Telescope.* "A remarkable book, worth much to thoughtful people."—*Pastor T. H. B. Anderson.* "A graphic and powerful representation of the author's interpretation."—*Michigan Christian Advocate.* "It is by a vigorous thinker and pungent writer. It is worthy a thoughtful and prayerful perusal."—*Guide to Holiness.*"

OTHER BOOKS BY THIS AUTHOR.

Victory ....25c.	Spiritual Gifts and
Holy Land...........40c.	Graces...........25c.
Sanctification.........25c.	Christian Perfection....25c.
Holiness or Hell.......30c.	The Woman Preacher..10c.

FOUR COPIES OF ANY SET FOR THE PRICE OF ONLY THREE.

The Sanctified Life

PRICE, $1.00.

It shows people how to recover sanctification if lost, and how to keep it and never lose it. It illuminates, assists, strengthens, and settles and confirms them in the sanctified life.

THE BETTER WAY, - - 75 cts.

CONTENTS: 1. Opening Words. 2. The Better Redemption. 3. The Better Prayer. 4. The Better Hope. 5. The More Excellent Sacrifice. 6. The Better Covenant. 7. A Better Experience. 8. A Better Supping. 9. The More Excellent Way. 10. A Better Life. 11. A Deeper Salvation. 12. A Greater Privilege. 13. The Better Resurrection. 14. The Abundant Entrance into Heaven. 15. The Better Reward at the Judgment. 16. The Better Company in Heaven. 17. The Higher Grade in Eternity. 18. How to Enter. 19. Paul's Way. 20. The Saviour's Way. 21. The Methodist Way. 22. Witnesses in Wesley's Days. 23. Witnesses in Our Time. 24. How I Entered In.

The Ram's Horn: "A BIBLE GALLERY of BEAUTIFUL PICTURES of the better way."
Northern Christian Advocate: "His style is fresh and vigorous, and spirit most commendable."
The Author: "I think this book will be more convincing and effective in bringing people into the blessing of sanctification than any other book I have written."

Post-paid, 75c. Agents wanted. Write for special rates by the quantity.

Other Books by Bro. Carradine.—Sanctification, 80c.; The Second Blessing in Symbol, $1.00; A Journey to Palestine, $1.50; The Bottle, 25c.; Twenty Objections to Church Entertainments, 50c.; The Old Man, $1.00; Pastoral Sketches, $1.00; Sermons, $1.00.

ORDER OF THIS OFFICE.

Full Salvation Library.

Books by Martin Wells Knapp.

86,000 ISSUED.

Lightning Bolts from Pentecostal Skies;
Or, Devices of the Devil Unmasked.

Table of Contents.

FRONTISPIECE OF AUTHOR.

I., Lightning Bolts; II., The Pentecostal Baptism; III., Pentecostal Sanctification; IV., Pentecostal Conversions; V., Pentecostal Revivals; VI., Pentecostal Homes; VII., Pentecostal Gifts; VIII., Pentecostal Giving; IX., Pentecostal Healing; X., Pentecostal Expectancy of Christ's Return; XI., The Pentecostal Church; XII., Pentecostal Preachers; XIII., Pentecostal Impostors.

Striking Illustrations designed by Author;

Executed by J. A. Knapp.

1. Struck by Lightning. 2. Lost, Saved, Fully Sanctified. 3. Diagram of Christ's Return. 4. The Rapture. 5. On the Rock and on the Sand. 6. "Three Demon Spirits Hover."

Neatly bound, Over 300 pages **READ IT ! HEED IT !** Good paper Price, $1.00

Other Books by this Author.

Out of Egypt Into Canaan. 24,000. 80 cents. "Able clear, and forcible."—Central Methodist.

Christ Crowned Within. 19,000. 75 cents. "A treasury of the burning thoughts of those who lived nearest the master."—Bishop McCabe.

Impressions. 6,000. 50 cents. "A most instructive, suggestive and useful book."--S. A. Keen. "We advise everybody to read it."—Central Baptist.

The Double Cure. Sanctification simplified. 13,000. New edition, 40 cents. Paper, 10 cents.

Revival Kindlings. Revival facts and incidents. 6,000. $1.00. "It will be read with comfort and delight."—Mich. Christian Advocate.

Revival Tornadoes. 13,000. $1.00. "A keen exposure of sham revivals."—Christian Standard.

The River of Death. For the young. 50 cents. Paper, 15 cents.

ORDER OF THIS OFFICE.

CHOICE BOOKLETS.

FROM INGERSOLL PARK TO BEULAH LAND. Experience of Rev. E. P. Brown, the converted infidel editor, and now chief editor of "The Ram's Horn." Over 50,000 circulated. One minister writes: "I think it's grand. I wept and shouted while I read it." Another: "I believe it the best tract I know of to give to hardened sinners;" and another says: "They go like fire." 10c.

THE BLOOD CURE FOR THE TOBACCO APPETITE. Arranged and partially composed by the Editor of The Revivalist. 20c per dozen; $1 per 100.

WOMEN PREACHERS. Reasons why women should preach. Rev. W. B. Godbey. Splendid. 10c.

JUDAS ISCARIOT: His Relation to Christ and Christian Experience. A striking Holiness sermon. 10c; 15 copies, $1.

THE REVIVAL AT SAMARIA: or, The First Work and the Second. A stirring Revival discourse. 10c; 15 copies, $1. This and Judas Iscariot by Rev. C. J. Fowler, President of the National Holiness Association.

HOLDING OUT. By Edgar P. Ellyson, minister of the Friends Church. "Just the thing for young converts." Both well written and well made. Cloth, 35c.

BEAUTY FOR ASHES; or, Heart Wanderings: Their Cause and Cure. A neat booklet, by the author of "Coals of Fire," "White Robes," "Holiness Manual," etc. 10c; $1 per dozen.

SOME GRAPES FROM ESCHOL. A Sermon on Perfect Love, by Rev. J. L. Glascock; also, his Christian Experience. The grapes are fresh, fragrant, and sweet. 25c.

ST. PAUL ON HOLINESS. 10c.

THE HOLY DAY. Pickett. 10c.

VALUABLE TRACTS.

GOSPEL ARROWS. Sentence questions and texts for the unconverted. 10c per 100.

WHAT SIN IS DESTROYING YOUR SOUL? A pungent, convictive tract for the unconverted. 5c per dozen; 25c per 100.

DANCING DANGER SIGNALS. Thirty-two facts against dancing. 25c per 100.

FORTY FACTS AGAINST CHURCH FESTIVALS, and sixty in favor of God's plan. 8c per dozen; 30c per 100.

REVIVAL HAND-BILLS. 30c per 100.

MARRIAGE ALARM BELLS. 8c per dozen; 30c per 100. One lady says: "It is worth $5." A valuable advisor for the young.

LETTER PAPER AND ENVELOPES. With signet and texts. 8c per dozen; 30c per 100.

Soul Food Library.

By G. D. WATSON.

1. Soul Food.   Price, 50 Cts.   Four Copies, $1.

Full of luminous matter on the following subjects: The Daily Cross: A Deeper Death to Self; Our Need of Humanity; Alone with God; Lukewarmness; The Fruit of Temptation; Sorrow for Sin; Loquacity; Let God; Simplicity; Little Things; Burdens of Prayer; Fretting Over Ourselves; Into the Deep; Feeding Our Faith; Personal Love of Jesus; Benefit of Deep Crucifixion; Loaded Words; The Dominant Soul Quality.

Rev. B. Carradine, writing of it, says, "I have read a number of the works of this gifted man, but the last is, to my mind, his most spiritual book and his best."

Pastor C. O. Isaac, of M. E. Church, Baltimore, Md., writes, "It is worth its weight in gold."

The Wesleyan Methodist: "The book, in our opinion, sustains to deeply spiritual truth, much the same relation that Joseph Cook's Boston Monday Lectures sustain to metaphysical truth."

2. Beauty for Ashes.   Price, 10 Cents.

Full of warnings against heart wanderings from God and encouragement to restoration.   With original poems on the Holy Spirit.

3. Types of the Holy Spirit. Price, 10 Cts.

4. Pure Gold.   Price, 50 Cents.

Being select essays on real saintliness of character.   Heart-searching and inspiring.

5. Love Abounding.   Price, $1.00.

Containing sermons reported just as delivered.

6. White Robes.   Price, 50 Cents.

This book gives clear definitions of the differences between cleansing and growth, mixed and unmixed love, etc.

7. Coals of Fire.   Price, 50 Cents.

Contains very thoughtful expositions of the perfection of faith and the Christian graces from the Old Testament.   A spiritual classic.

8. Secret of Spiritual Power.   Price, 50 Cents.

Treats of the union of the Holy Spirit with the human soul.

9. Holiness Manual.   Price, 25 Cents.

Containing twenty-five Bible readings describing the stages of grace, with proof texts.

M. W. KNAPP, REVIVALIST OFFICE, CINCINNATI, O.

CLOTH EDITION.

OUT OF EGYPT INTO CANAAN;

OR,
Lessons in Spiritual Geography. | BY ...
Martin Wells Knapp.

28,000 ISSUED. PRICE, 80 CENTS.

CONTENTS:

ILLUSTRATIVE MAP: In Egypt, or Spiritual Bondage—The Red Sea, or Spiritual Deliverance—The Sinai Wilderness, or Spiritual Twilight—Kadesh-Barnea, or the Believers' Waterloo—Desert Wilderness, or "Wretched Religion"—Entering Canaan—Canaan, or Spiritual Sunshine—Out of Canaan into Babylon—Back from Babylon—Out of Canaan into Heaven—Canaan Contrasts and Inquiries—The Author's Experience.

KIND COMMENTS.

Adapted.—We do not hesitate to pronounce this book well adapted to the instruction of the people in divine things. It cannot help being useful.—*Christian Witness.*

Original.—Its method of presentation is original. It is well written, and worthy of extensive circulation.—*Christian Standard and Home Journal.*

Striking.—The author's style abounds in illustrations of the thoughts he wishes to give stress, which are apt, and at times striking.—*Wesleyan Christian Advocate.*   )

Able.—It is an able, clear, and forcible statement of the higher-life doctrine.—*Central Methodist.*

Crowded.—Crowded full of choice instruction and counsel. * * * We cannot too highly commend the design of the work, nor the manner in which the design is executed.—*Wesleyan Methodist.*

Encouraging.—Volume contains much of instruction and encouragement to all who will live godly.—*Western Christian Advocate.*

Next to His Bible.—If I ever write an article on "Books that have helped me," I am sure that next to the Bible I must place your "Out of Egypt."—*Rev. T. H. Murlin.*

Vigorous.—This volume is well written in an original style. It ends with the interesting personal experience of the author.—*David D. Updegraff, Mount Pleasant, O.*

Salable.—Please send me sixteen books. I took orders for them in less than three hours.—*O. F. Winget, Stanfordville, N. Y.*

A Good Evangelist.—I just keep it going around among the people. One person was saved and sanctified through the reading of it. I would like to give it to every young convert.—*John McFarland, Stoneham, Mass.*

SPECIAL RATES BY THE QUANTITY.

Pentecostal Light,

By REV. A. M. HILLS.

---

101 Large Pages.   Price in Cloth, 50 Cents.
In Paper Cover, 10 Cents.

THIS BOOK TREATS OF:

"Praying for the Spirit.   Filled with the Spirit.
Grieve not the Spirit."

IT HAS HAD A CIRCULATION OF OVER THREE
THOUSAND IN TWELVE MONTHS.

Rev. S. T. Morris, of Calumet, Mich., writes:
"Pentecostal Light is a work of power, and should be in the hands of every believer in America. It is rightly named, and you have my special thanks for writing it."
"The last chapter alone is worth its price."
"Effective medicine for worldliness among professors.

Address M. W. KNAPP, Revivalist Office,

CINCINNATI, OHIO.

Life and Labors of Mary A. Woodbridge,

By REV. A. M. HILLS.

LARGE. BEAUTIFULLY BOUND. 406 PAGES. PRICE, $1.50.

Mrs. Woodbridge was for six years President of Ohio W. C. T. U., for seventeen years, Recording Secretary of National W. C. T. U., and later, Corresponding Secretary of World's and National Woman's Christian Temperance Union.

The following are a few of fifty notices of this book:

FRANCES E. WILLARD: "We have received the beautiful book about Mary and rejoice that it is a record so adequate of a life so genial, healthful, and complete. . . . If it could be read by the young women in our Sunday-schools, King's Daughter Circles, Endeavorers, Leagues, and Colleges, the outcome would be a band of rare recruits for the White-Ribbon army. I hope the book will meet with the reception it deserves, and become a standard in the homes of good people throughout many nations. . . . LADY SOMERSET joins me in the expression of the highest commendation."

MRS. SUSANNA M. D. FRY, PH. D., State President Minnesota W. C. T. U.: "The book is beautiful in form, beautiful in material excellency, but most noticeably beautiful in that which is highest and best, the Spirit, the thought, and sentiment of the book."

MISS E. M. FRANCIS, Providence, R. I., Editor of *Outlook*: "It is a precious book and many will want it."

DR. SIMEON GILBERT, Editor *Times-Herald*, Chicago: "The book is admirably prepared, and is one of extraordinary interest. It is such a book as one wishes may have the widest possible circulation."

Union Signal: "No book could bring more comfort to a Christian well in years, and none could more safely instruct and encourage a beginner in the religious life."

ELLEN D. MORRIS, Kansas City, Mo.: "A copy should be in every Sunday-school library."

ORDER OF══════

M. W. KNAPP, Cincinnati, O.

FOOD FOR LAMBS;

OR,

LEADING CHILDREN TO CHRIST.

By A. M. Hills,

Author of "Holiness and Power" and "Pentecostal Light."

Abridged Edition.

Price, 10 Cents; 16 for $1.00.

TABLE OF CONTENTS—Chapter I., Why God Calls Children Early; II., Same—Continued; III., Same—Continued; IV., Two Other Reasons Why God Calls Little Children to Remember Him and Seek Him; V., First Condition of Salvation—Repentance; VI., The Second Condition of Salvation—Faith; VII., The Third Condition of Salvation—Surrender of Self to God's Service; VIII., Coming to Christ.

Complete Edition.

Price, Cloth, 80 Cents; 4 Copies, $2.40.

TABLE OF CONTENTS—Chapter I., Why God Calls Children Early; II., Same—Continued; III., Same—Continued; IV., Two Other Reasons Why God Calls Little Children to Remember Him and Seek Him; V., First Condition of Salvation—Repentance; VI, The Second Condition of Salvation—Faith; VII., The Third Condition of Salvation—Surrender of Self to God's Service; VIII., Coming to Christ; IX., Ten Evidences of Conversion; X., Prayer; XI., The Bible; XII., Obedience; XIII., A Life of Love; XIV., A Life of Service; XV., Joining the Church; XVI., Religion Made Easy by the Holy Ghost.

This is an invaluable and timely Text-Book for training Children in the Home, Sunday-School and Day School.

No Parent or Teacher can Afford to be Without it.

Free from cant and adapted to believers of every name. It will help fasten truth in the child-mind as no other book we know.

The 80-cent Book and The Weekly Revivalist,
One Year, $1.50.

ORDER OF THIS OFFICE.

OLD CORN.

BY

DAVID B. UPDEGRAFF.

TABLE OF CONTENTS.

Price, $1.00; Four Copies, prepaid, $3.00.

It and THE REVIVALIST, weekly, one year, $1.75.

Send all orders to

M. W. KNAPP,

REVIVALIST OFFICE, CINCINNATI, OHIO.

FOR ONLY 35 CENTS

YOU CAN GET

Tears and Triumphs Combined

CONTAINING THE

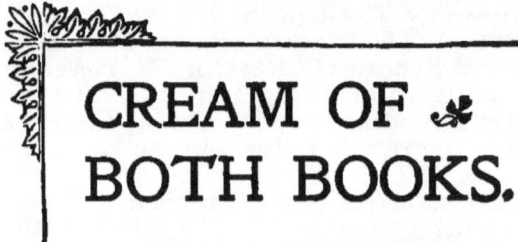

CREAM OF ❧
BOTH BOOKS.

SEND 35 CENTS FOR SAMPLE.

❧ Special Rates by the Quantity. ❧

IN MUSLIN, 30 CENTS.

ORDER OF THIS OFFICE.

www.ingramcontent.com/pod-product-compliance
Lightning Source LLC
Chambersburg PA
CBHW021113020726
47500CB00003B/741